W9-CHQ-830

Serita lay in the dark with her eyes open. She couldn't sleep.

She couldn't stop reliving the way Hunter kissed her. She couldn't get over how she felt at this moment just thinking about him. He was kind, funny, intelligent, ambitious, gorgeous, sexy….

Finally, Serita drifted off into a pleasant dream. In it, Hunter entered her bedroom and approached her. Then suddenly, a dark energy invaded her reverie. Hunter vanished from her dream and in his place, a man with a ski mask stood over her. Moaning with dread because of the horrible but familiar nightmare, Serita woke sweating, restless and frightened. The last time she had this dream was the night her husband had been murdered.

Rehashing it all made Serita afraid. She started to call out to Hunter, but decided against that. She wouldn't cling to the first man since her husband who made her feel like he cared about her. But somehow, Hunter didn't make her feel only as if he cared, he made her feel much more….

LOURÉ BUSSEY

is the author of *Nightfall, Most of All, Twist of Fate, Love So True, A Taste of Love, Images of Ecstasy, Dangerous Passions, Just the Thought of You, If Loving You Is Wrong* and *Tropical Heat*. Her books have appeared on Ingram's and Amazon's bestseller lists. She is also a business owner and singer/songwriter. Her debut CD *Dreams Do Come True* is scheduled to be released in 2006.

Louré Bussey

Secretly in Love

If you purchased this book without a cover you should be aware
that this book is stolen property. It was reported as "unsold and
destroyed" to the publisher, and neither the author nor the
publisher has received any payment for this "stripped book."

To Brandon Christopher,
With all my love
Louré Bussey

 KIMANI PRESS™

ISBN-13: 978-1-58314-785-6
ISBN-10:   1-58314-785-3

SECRETLY IN LOVE

Copyright © 2006 by Louré Bussey

All rights reserved. The reproduction, transmission or utilization
of this work in whole or in part in any form by any electronic, mechanical
or other means, now known or hereafter invented, including xerography,
photocopying and recording, or in any information storage or retrieval
system, is forbidden without written permission. For permission please
contact Kimani Press, Editorial Office, 233 Broadway, New York, NY
10279 U.S.A.

All characters in this book have no existence outside the imagination of
the author and have no relation whatsoever to anyone bearing the same
name or names. They are not even distantly inspired by any individual
known or unknown to the author, and all incidents are pure invention.
Any resemblance to actual persons, living or dead, is entirely coincidental.

® and TM are trademarks. Trademarks indicated with ® are registered in
the United States Patent and Trademark Office, the Canadian Trade Marks
Office and/or other countries.

www.kimanipress.com

Printed in U.S.A.

Dear Reader,

Thank you for sharing this journey of love with me. I hope that Serita and Hunter's story reminded you of how magical finding a soul mate can be. I'm a romantic. I believe that there is someone for everyone, and that by God's design, each of us is making our way closer to that special person we were intended to be with. I also believe that when you least expect it, your dream comes true.

I am so grateful for the e-mails, cards and letters that I receive from readers. They are beautiful gifts and surprises that I treasure. Please feel free to contact me at LoureBus@aol.com, or Louré Bussey, c/o Blue Nile Entertainment, LLC, Newport Financial Center, 113 Pavonia Avenue, #638, Jersey City, New Jersey 07310-1756.

God Bless you all, and may all your dreams come.

Louré Bussey

Chapter 1

Madera Bay looked lush, green and sea beautiful as Serita Jones gave a tour of her South Carolina home to the man she had met and married within three months. Aside from the stares from town's people who had nothing better to do than to gossip about her family and the scandal that had plagued her life, Serita found the ride around the island enjoyable. So did her husband, Chris.

She had met him at her friend Lauren's wedding reception in New York. As a bridesmaid at the ceremony, Serita smiled and gussied up in a lovely, pink gown, and hid that her heart broke every second because her father died two weeks before the wedding. Mingling with Lauren's family and friends and fending off the flirts, she wandered toward a lounge where she thought she left her bouquet. As soon as she walked in the room, she heard a guy holler out, "That's my beautiful wife right there."

Startled, Serita looked aside to see who declared such a thing. A group of men huddled together smiling at her. One of them walked her way. Of medium stature and thirty-something, he had dark, luminous eyes, short hair and a wide smile made unforgettable because of the grape-deep dimples that accentuated it.

"I'm Chris," he introduced himself and pecked her knuckles with his soft lips. "When I saw you come down the aisle, I knew I had to meet you. And I meant what I just said, you will be my beautiful wife. I don't know how I know that, but I just do."

Serita felt a tingle on her hand and as well felt tickled by him. He had to be the flirtiest man of the night. Yet it was all right. She knew not to take him seriously—she had made that mistake with someone else. It had ended in heartbreak of another kind, just before her father passed. With this attractive stranger, she planned simply to enjoy the moment.

But Chris stole more than a moment of her time. Serita and he danced on the up-tempo songs and had a spectacular time doing so. They created some smooth footwork on the floor that had his buddies cheering him on and Lauren giving her the thumbs up. They also moved together on the slow grinds. Their bodies pressed so close that they had to step outside and get some air from the heat that stirred up between them. Out there cooling off, Serita let him heat her up again with a kiss.

As his lips melded with hers and his arms swept around her, a lusty ache grew in the pit of Serita's belly. It enticed her to slip her arms around his solid body and thank God for such delicious surprises. It had been a long time since something made her feel so good instead of so sad.

Serita postponed driving back to Madera Bay. Chris begged her to hang around so they could get more acquainted. She desired the same.

Besides, all that awaited her on the island was the lonesome house she had shared with her father and the business she had closed because she had to care for him.

New York City then became her wonderland of fun and passion. During a whirlwind courtship of wining and dining, and indulging in all sorts of pleasures, she came to know Chris Johnson. In addition to being the owner of a small carpentry and construction business, he was a man that warmed her heart with laughter, kindness and affection. Whenever she cried about her father, she had strong arms to hold her. Whenever life blessed her with something beautiful, she could share it with someone.

After Chris proposed and they eloped at New York's City Hall, all during a three-month time frame, Lauren questioned Serita about her hasty marriage. After all, Lauren had known Chris only six months herself. Her fiancé, now husband, Damien, had hired Chris to do cabinet-making on the new home they'd purchased. Though Chris seemed wonderful, Lauren expressed reservations about Serita pledging a lifelong commitment to a man she barely knew.

Serita argued that she did know Chris. In the three months she had spent with him, it felt like she knew him better than people she knew her entire life.

Now, they had come to the island to take care of her business affairs and to let Chris get the feel of Madera Bay. Undecided about where they wanted to reside, they weighed the pros and cons of the island and New York. Though the wavering wasn't a problem. Since Chris could operate his business at any location, and Serita intended to start a new one that allowed her flexibility in the locale, they could pursue their dreams anywhere.

Winding up their island sightseeing, Serita drove Chris to her favorite hotspot, a secluded section of Madera Bay Beach. Since they had planned to laze at the oceanside, they wore swimsuits underneath their clothes. Hence, once Serita parked her Ford Explorer, they shed their casual gear. Seconds later, their bare feet made imprints in the sand. The white-beige grains sparkled like chopped diamonds beneath the blazing, southern sun.

Feeling playful, she ran ahead of Chris. She

liked the way his eyes adored her in her skimpy, red bikini. Due to the stress of her father's illness coupled with a love affair gone awry, she had eaten too much and gained a little weight. It made her self-conscious until Chris told her he liked a little meat on his women, especially in the hip area where her extra clung.

She also liked that he kept complimenting the way the color accentuated her deep, brown complexion. It all made her feel beautiful, something she hadn't felt in a long, long time.

Teasing him with provocative sways of her hips, she lured him to chase her. Serita laughed loudly as she dashed through the sand. The sound mingled with the swish of waves crashing against the shore.

Eventually Chris caught up to her while the ocean water circled her knees. His well-built arms sealed her against him and he kissed Serita hungrily. As he caressed his way around to the back of her bikini top and began to untie it, Serita granted him a flirtatious look.

"Now, if you want that you're going to have to work for it." She backed away, drifting further into the sea.

Chris's dimples flashed at her. "Just for teasing me, I'm going to catch you and make you pay."

"I don't think you can," Serita taunted him.

"Don't think I can what?"

"Catch me, maybe. Make me pay, that's up to opinion." Laughing, she swam away.

Chris swam after her. "Girl, I'm going to bite that juicy bottom when I catch you."

He caught Serita within a second. They kissed and discovered a shady place on the shore to make love. After many steamy moments, they were spent and dozed off.

Moments later, Serita woke inhaling the salty, sea air. Yet that wasn't all that she became aware of when she awakened. She saw Chris swimming. She also heard footsteps and sensed a presence behind her—a presence that made her feel strange, even frightened.

When Serita whirled around to see if anyone else had visited this remote section of the beach, no one approached her. She found it peculiar. During the entire week since her return to Madera Bay, she had had similar experiences. Once in her backyard, she swore she heard

someone creeping up behind her. Outside her
bedroom window at night, she believed she
heard rustling in the bushes and footsteps.
Another time when she took out the trash, she
thought she saw a dark figure of a man that
hurried toward her from a distance. Until, that
is, Chris walked out the door. The menacing
looking vision vanished.

Chris investigated every instance for her. No
one appeared to be there. Serita decided she
wouldn't bother him about the weird sensation
that she just had. Perhaps it all had to do with
grieving. Her friend and neighbor, Mrs.
McFee, claimed that grief played a lot of
strange tricks on the mind. Maybe she just
missed her father too much.

Other than that alternative, what else could it
have been? Since she was far from rich, no one
should have gone out of his way to rob her.
Neither had she done anything to anyone on the
island or elsewhere for someone to want to harm
her. On the other hand, friends of hers had expressed more than once that she was justified in
feeling malice toward the people who had per-
secuted her family.

* * *

Miles away in Cedar Falls, Virginia, Hunter Larimore hammered into a piece of sheetrock in his friend Rick's garage. They had been great friends since Hunter purchased a five-bedroom home in the posh community of Emerald Hills a few years ago. That's when he met Rick, his neighbor across the street.

Now that Rick had fallen on difficult financial times and taken a consultant position in Norway, Hunter wanted to help his buddy out. Whenever Rick's wife, Giselle, mentioned that she needed house repairs, Hunter volunteered to do the work. After all, as the owner of his own private airline service, and co-owner of other businesses, he created his own schedule. Since life had blessed him with so much, he enjoyed making his family and friends' lives easier by doing whatever he could. As well, he got a kick out of home repairing. It had become one of his hobbies.

"How is everything going in here?" Giselle asked, surprising Hunter. Flinging her long braids out of her face, she stepped into the garage clad in daisy duke shorts, a tank top and high heel mule sandals. She also handed Hunter a huge slice of strawberry cheesecake.

"Thank you," Hunter said, lying the hammer down and accepting the cheesecake. He took a bite. His facial expression revealed how delicious the cake was. "My goodness, that's tasty! You can bake, girl! And this is my favorite dessert!"

"I know." Giselle granted him a smile, which showed both rows of her perfect teeth. "I remember you saying that one day when you visited Rick."

Hunter's brown eyes widened with surprise. "You remember that?"

"I remember a lot about you, Hunter." She stepped toward him, raking her catlike eyes over the muscles revealed from his white T-shirt. They looked like suntanned-brown grapefruits stacked on top of one another.

Hunter caught her eye action and chewed his cake a little slower. Suddenly he felt like a piece of meat, just the way women described themselves feeling at times. Yet he had to be imagining that he received that vibe from his good friend's wife. Rick and Giselle seemed like one of the happiest couples he had ever known. And he hadn't known many. Surely, she wouldn't try to flirt with her husband's buddy and neighbor.

"Hunter," Giselle continued, gliding her nail over his arm. "I think you're a gorgeous man. And not just gorgeous, I think you're damn sexy—so sexy I could eat a piece of you."

Hunter choked on a piece of cake and coughed. Giselle patted his back until he stopped.

"Thank you," he said, clearing his throat.

She beamed. "You were really going at that food. I bet you go at everything like that—like it's the last time you'll get a piece."

Hunter cleared his throat again. "It's good cake."

"I have more than good cake."

"Yes, you're a great cook. I always tell Rick that."

"I cook in all kinds of ways. And I think we would heat up something real good together."

"Really," he remarked, clearing his throat again.

"You know something I heard about you?"

"Uh, what?" he asked almost scared to hear her answer.

"Your next door neighbor, Dawn, she's always telling me about how you have those

women hollering over in your house at night—
that good kind of hollering." Pausing, she rolled
her tongue around her lips. "She hears through
your open windows. She says she can only
imagine what you're doing to them."

Hunter's brows rose with surprise at this
news. "She imagines that, huh?"

"Oh, yes! But I don't want to hear any second-
hand descriptions." She poked his chest lightly.
"I want to know firsthand what you're doing to
them. Because I know it's something good. You
turn me on just looking at you. You turned me
on since you first moved on the block."

Slowly Hunter backed away from Giselle and
questioned the reality of this moment. His friend's
wife had turned into a wild seductress ready to
jump his bones. What made this situation so uncomfortable was that he had had sexual fantasies
about Giselle in the past. He knew it was wrong,
but they sneaked through his mind anyway. She
was an attractive woman, with curves in all the
places he liked, and she had a sexy voice.

Even so, just because he had lusty thoughts
about a woman didn't mean he had to get buck
wild with her between the sheets. Several times

when he had driven his car and another driver cut him off, he had wanted to jump out of his vehicle and choke the other driver senseless. Yet he didn't do it because it was wrong. It was a thought. Seducing Giselle was a thought, too. And that's all it would ever be.

"Giselle," he said, his tall physique retreating a little further. "That's not me. I don't sleep with my friend's wives."

"Ah, don't be worried about Rick. I'll never tell."

"That's not it."

"Then what is it?" Giselle came at him, backing him against the wall, palming his broad, solid chest. "What is it, sexy?"

Gently Hunter forced her hands down at her side. "It's just not right."

"But I've seen the way you look at me."

Hunter looked away, not realizing he had been so obvious.

Studying his face, Giselle laughed. "Oh, so you have been thinking about us getting busy?"

Hunter swallowed and wiped beads of perspiration that popped across his forehead and thought, *Giselle, I'm a man. We think about sex all the time—all the time! And I may think about it much more than most. In fact, I'm sure I do. But I'm not a dog.*

"Look, Giselle," he said, feeling a bit breathless, "sexing up friends' wives is not my style. I'm sorry."

On that note, Hunter gathered his tools and got a move on out of the garage. When he glanced over his shoulder at Giselle, her arms were folded and her eyes burned into his skin.

"I'm sorry," he uttered again. "I'll just forget this, and I hope you do the same."

When Hunter returned to his house, he showered and tried to take a nap. He expected a date later. He couldn't stop thinking about Giselle and Rick. As hard as that man worked to give that woman the best in life, and as well as Rick treated Giselle, she had the nerve to come on to his friend. Did she love him? Did she even care? Did she ever imagine how it would feel if Rick betrayed her in the same way?

Hunter pitied Rick. He pitied others he knew, too. Love and marriage just complicated life.

From what he had seen, marriages hardly ever worked out.

His parents were the only two people he knew who truly loved each other and honored their marriage vows into their senior years. Sure, they'd had little spats from time to time. Half the time they clashed about raising five overly energetic boys and two daddy's girls. The other quarrels were due to the financial troubles they'd endured until their father's business became an overwhelming success. Overall, his parents showed him what real love looked like.

As for everyone else, through the test of time the love always perished. Certainly, he knew couples that had been married until their silver and gold anniversaries. His aunts, uncles and friends' parents had reached such milestones. But what was the point of being together when they always looked at their spouse as if they could kill him—or hated to come home to them and get nagged to death—or simply hopped in bed with any other willing partner that crossed their path.

Worse, things always became ugly when a couple parted ways. So many of his buddies battled nasty divorces, fighting over children, money and possessions and grew to hate the spouse they once cherished. Their existence was a constant state of hell due to the one they had vowed to love. Why put yourself through all that? He never would.

And indeed, he felt happy for his two brothers, Jackson and Randall, who recently married. He hoped for the best for them. Though with the track record of other marriages he had seen, in time, he suspected they would march to a divorce court.

Due to all the headaches and near heart attacks caused by uttering those three words *I love you*, and the other four, *Will you marry me*, Hunter never dared to speak them. Long ago, he had decided neither was for him. Now, at age forty-four, his mind had not changed. What's more, he always told women right from the start that he did not intend to fall in love and did not intend to marry—ever.

At dawn the next morning, Serita tossed in her bed with her eyes shut tight. *She and Chris had horsed around on the beach at night. That is, until she treated herself to a swim. Soon after, she heard a moan at the shore and beheld Chris bending over until he collapsed. A hulking, faceless figure that had hurt him hurried toward her in the black sea.*

Waking from the nightmare, Serita sprang up against the headboard and cradled her face with her palms. When Chris's eyes fluttered open and he saw her, he pulled her close to his chest.

"What's wrong?" he asked, nipping her chin. "A bad dream?"

"Yes."

"So what was it about?"

Serita hesitated in answering. She disliked sharing her dreams. She especially disliked sharing them with someone who she dreamed about in which something frightening happened to them.

"It was nothing."

"Nothing sure had you upset."

"It was just me in a crazy situation."

"What do you mean crazy?"

She shrugged her shoulders. "A dangerous one."

"How so?"

"Oh, baby, it's nothing." She patted his arm.

"Was I in it?"

"Uh, I think so."

He was quiet for a moment. "It was about me, wasn't it? Something bad happened to me and you don't want to tell me about it. That's it, isn't it?"

"Really, it was nothing."

"Serita," he whispered, snuggling her tighter against him. "It was just a dream. You can tell me. I'm your husband. We should share everything. I share everything with you."

Serita thought for a moment. "All right. I...I dreamed that we were at the beach at night and this brute hurt you and came after me."

"So what? It was just a dream."

"It was a nightmare. And the last time I had one, it was about my dad standing on a highway at night, disappearing into a fog. Next night he had that massive heart attack and died."

"But I'm sure you've had nightmares and nothing happened."

Serita pondered that. "Yes, I have." Her plump lips curved into a smile. "You always know how to calm me."

"That's all I know how to do?" Chris leaned

over her and kissed her passionately. When he released her, he sighed with satisfaction. "You keep driving me crazy like that and I'm not getting out of this bed. I'll forget about going shopping."

"We can forget it if you want. If you don't feel like it, it's fine."

"No, I was just kidding. I'm supposed to take my lady shopping today and I will. I want you to get the sexiest dress there is to wear on that party boat tonight."

At noon, Detective Mitchell Lane dined at an outside table at Lovett's café. It was a popular restaurant in Madera Bay's shopping district. As he munched on a Lovett's hero special that he found scrumptious, his dark eyes captured a sight across the street that made him stop chewing and lose his appetite.

Accompanied by an unfamiliar man, Serita strode along the sidewalk. The stranger carried shopping bags, while they laughed, talked and window-shopped. Mitchell couldn't miss the way the sunlight shimmered on her rich, brown skin tone, accentuating her African-American and Blackfoot Indian descent. Her exotic, slanted eyes sparkled with happiness. Her long, black, wavy hair blew with the island's gentle breeze. And her curvaceous body swayed sinuously in a pale, pink sundress that showed off bare, oiled, shapely legs.

Mitchell stared and stared until he felt eyes on him. Aware that he had rudely ignored his wife, Julie, because of his attention to another woman, he turned to her.

Julie's thin, russet-painted lips spread into a vibrant smile. "They make a nice couple, don't they?" She threw her head full of auburn hair toward Serita and the man who walked with her. "I heard she married him after knowing him only three months."

"Is that right?" Mitchell bit into his sandwich and avoided looking across the street.

"Yes, that's what I heard." Julie's light brown eyes trailed the lovers. "Must be love. I can't wait for us to renew our vows and show everyone that our love has only grown over the years." Perfectly manicured fingers clutched Mitchell's hand.

He forced a smile and continued eating his sandwich.

"If daddy wasn't so sick," she went on, "I'd renew them today."

Mitchell mused on her words while he chewed that last portion of his hero. When he had eaten it all, he glimpsed his watch, pecked her on the cheek and stood.

Julie's face sank with disappointment. "Aw, you're leaving so soon?"

"It's time for me to get back to the station. I'm working on an interesting case."

Julie looked tickled. "On this island? Nothing ever happens here, thank God."

"Things do happen here. And something major happened here in the past."

"Like what?"

"It's an old case I'm looking into. I'm determined to solve it."

"What old case? I've lived here all my life and I can't think of any unsolved crime."

"Don't worry. I'll let you know about it in time."

"Well, don't let it make you late for tonight. I'm really excited about this party boat coming to the island and I can't wait to have a good time with you there tonight."

"I'll be there with you."

"You better, Mr. Mysterious," Mitchell heard Julie utter as he strode away. Once he made his way farther down the street, he glimpsed back toward Serita and her new husband. He wondered what she would think if she knew the case he looked into involved her.

In the evening Serita stood in her bathroom with a large white towel wrapped around her freshly bathed body. Taking her time, she rubbed a peach scented body cream on her skin when she heard a thump outside her window. She glanced out the window and saw nothing. Was she hearing things? It made her wonder if she needed to see a doctor. Maybe she needed a medication for her nerves. She had seen them advertised on television a lot lately.

Chris strolled into the bathroom and took a deep breath of her fruity scent. "Umm, I might have to take you to bed right now smelling like that."

Serita eyed him with an entrancing smile. "What are you trying to do? Kill me?"

"If you want to call it that, but you'll have to wait for later. I promised you dancing on a yacht and that's what we're going to do. I want to spoil you." He pulled her against him and wrapped his arms around her small waist. "These last years all you did was take care of your dad."

"I didn't mind. I wish I could still take care of him."

"You did everything a daughter could do and, in the midst of it all, a fool broke your heart."

Serita tensed up with the mention of her other heartbreak. "I don't want to talk about him."

Over an hour later, Serita and Chris boarded the *San Clavita* party yacht. After dancing nonstop to several up-tempo R&B hits, Chris headed to get them some refreshments at a jam-packed bar. Serita saw the lengthy line and decided to stroll around the ship while she waited for Chris. Eventually her tour led her to a secluded area of the boat and she leaned on its barrier. The location had a breathtaking view of Madera Bay, along with neighboring South Carolina islands. Inhaling the sea air, she simply savored the moment.

"How are you?" she heard a familiar, mascu-line voice inquire.

Serita looked to her left. Dressed in a dark

blue suit, Mitchell's tall, robust frame stepped toward her.

"I'm fine," Serita answered, not granting him the slightest smile. "And you?"

Mitchell stood next to her. His dark, scintillating eyes searched her face. "I'm all right. You look great."

"Thanks." Serita gazed out to sea.

Several seconds passed with him staring at her profile before he asked, "How is the newlywed life?"

"Wonderful. How is the married life?" She looked aside at him.

The moonlight shined on his handsome features crowned by short, curly hair. But Mitchell had no answer. Instead, he stared into her eyes so intensely that Serita grew uncomfortable. Thinking it was best to rejoin Chris, she walked away from the ship's edge. As she did, Mitchell grabbed her arm, halting her steps.

"Did you marry him because of me?"

Insulted, Serita jerked his hand off of her. "Sorry, Detective, you have this one figured wrong."

"But I heard you only knew him three months."

Serita shook her head at the way some on

the island gossiped. Because she had shared her good news about her sudden marriage with her beautician while other customers were present, she surmised that the story had spread around like wildfire. Her hairstylist, Naomi, had been genuinely happy for her. As for the others, who knew what people harbored in their hearts?

Some were probably elated for her. Others who had unfulfilled and miserable lives would make something ugly out of it because they were jealous.

"So you're a gossipmonger now, Mitchell?"

"I don't know about any gossip. I do know about you and me."

"There is no you and me. It's you and your wife—the wife you never told me about. You made me think you were a new, single guy in town and all along you're the husband Julie Branson brought back home with her."

"So you run off to New York and marry a guy you hardly know?"

"It had nothing to do with you. Sometimes a man and a woman just have a connection."

"I know."

With those words, Mitchell's eyes lingered on

hers. Serita observed him coldly for a second
and then walked away.

Hours later, Serita had returned from her night
on the town and stood in her kitchen cutting
potatoes. She wore Chris's shirt while he leaned
against the wall in his underwear admiring her.

"You're so damn beautiful," he said.

"And you're so greedy." She chuckled. "I
can't believe you have me making fries in the
dead of night."

"After what you did to me in that bed, I could
eat ten plates full."

"Sit down, lover boy. I'll have some hot stuff
ready in a few minutes."

"I'll be back in a minute," he said."

Chris left the kitchen, leaving Serita humming
and placing potatoes in the frying pan. He had
been gone only a few seconds when suddenly a
loud pop startled her. Coming from upstairs, it
sounded like a firecracker or even…a gunshot.
Serita cut off the stove's fire. Carefully she
walked out of the kitchen.

"Hey?" she yelled, stepping through the
living room. "What was that noise?"

She heard no answer.

"Chris? Are you okay?"

Silence again, so she mounted the stairs. Once she reached the upper floor, Serita inspected the bathroom. There was still no sight of Chris. So she stepped into the bedroom. She panned the cozy decor of floral patterns, and cherrywood furnishings, seeing no sight of him in there either. That is, until her heart jumped in her throat—she spotted his feet. From her angle, they stuck out from the bottom of the other side of the bed. With a gasp, Serita sped around to the opposite side.

With a better view, Serita grabbed her head. She felt as if she was suffocating. Chris was sprawled on the floor with blood oozing from his chest. Feeling outside her body, Serita heard her ear-piercing screams. Her heart hammered in her chest, ears and head, and she started bending down to help Chris. That's when arms grabbed her and swung her around. Before she saw the shooter's face, she felt a blast.

Chapter 2

There was a flurry of activity in front of Serita's home when Mitchell drove up. He had received the stunning call about shots fired at her home while resting in bed with Julie. After throwing on his clothes, he bolted out of the house and fled to the crime scene to ensure that Serita was okay. Now, seeing the commotion, he knew that she wasn't.

Rushing to her front door, he saw colleague's police cruisers, along with spectators crowding around the classic colonial two-level home. As he reached the porch, ambulance attendants carried out a covered body on a stretcher. His heartbeat felt as if it stopped.

He gestured to the attendants to halt while he lifted the cover up. The man who had accompanied Serita in the shopping district earlier in the day lay dead. Mitchell reeled in the shock for a moment. Afterward, he nodded to the attendants. They continued carrying the body out toward the ambulance. Mitchell entered the house. A thin, elderly lady with glasses ran up to him before he stepped inside.

"Aren't you the fellow that used to come by to see Serita?" she asked him in a feisty voice. "I'm Mrs. McFee, her neighbor."

"Yes, I am," Mitchell answered, his voice edged with impatience.

"I heard her screaming," Mrs. McFee rambled on, "blood curdling screams. I also heard the shots with the windows being open and all. So I called the police."

"I'm glad you did that."

"I heard it's too late for him and that's so sad. He seemed like such a nice fellow in the short time I knew him. But I pray and pray that it isn't too late for her. Serita is such a lovely girl."

"She certainly is."

Just then, ambulance attendants carried Serita outside on a stretcher. Unconscious, and with her head bandaged, oxygen masks covered her mouth and nose. Mitchell sighed with relief.

"Thank God she's alive," Mrs. McFee said, her hand clutching her chest. "Thank God!"

"And I'll make sure she stays alive," Mitchell added, following the stretcher.

In Cedar Falls, Virginia, Hunter gazed up at the pretty woman who had delighted him with all kinds of pleasurable tricks during the night. A flight attendant who he used to work with while employed as a pilot at a major airline, Janette never failed to amaze him. Their trysts didn't happen that often, but when they did, Hunter whistled happily for days afterward.

Now that their hot rendezvous had to end because she had to host a flight, Janette still tantalized him. She straddled him clad in a sexy, purple negligee that flaunted her voluptuous figure. Hunter raised his hands to cup her heart shaped face, then mingled his fingers in her wild, shoulder length mane.

"So I better get ready to go, my darling," she teased with a seductive curl of her lips.

"I wish you could stay."

"Maybe if you would make me an offer to stay permanently I would."

Hunter laughed her off. She had to be joking. Janette loved their arrangement—no strings, no stress and no complications. He admired her for being a confident woman who never smothered a man.

"I think about you often, Hunter, when I'm away," she elaborated. "I'm seeing another gentleman in Atlanta, but I'd drop him in a heartbeat if I could get a real commitment out of you."

"Are you serious?"

"Yes, I am." The playfulness faded from her voice. "I'm getting older and this date thing, or sex partners, or whatever it is we're doing is getting old, too. I want something more."

"I thought you enjoyed what we have."

"What do we have? We go out and have a good time. We even take trips to exotic locales in your private planes, and we always wind up making some real good loving. But there is more to life than that. And there is more to my feelings for you."

"Like what?" he whispered, coasting his hands along the sides of her waist.

"Like love. I love you, Hunter Larimore. And I think you love me, too, but for some reason, you just won't say it or even acknowledge it."

"Janette, I admit that I care about you deeply. You're one of the most wonderful and exciting women I've ever met. But I'm not ready for love or what comes with it."

"You mean marriage? Hunter, you're forty-four and I'm forty-two. Don't you think it's time for us to settle down?"

"Oh, I hate those words 'settling down.' It makes it sound like life is over, like all the fun is over."

"We can have more fun if we're committed to each other forever. Don't you want more? Don't you want happiness?"

"I'm very happy with my life."

"You are?" She scanned his bedroom, which looked large enough to install three other rooms in it. "Doesn't this big house get lonely when you're in it by yourself?"

"No. Actually, I love the quiet. With the huge family I grew up in, quiet time was a treasure."

Clearly frustrated, Janette shuffled off of him and sighed. "I give up then. And I better leave. And I mean for good."

He sat up. His handsome features etched with alarm. "What do you mean for good?"

"I mean the other fellow in Atlanta asked me to marry him. I really want to be with you. I really love you, but time is precious and I can't wait on you, Hunter."

Moments later, Janette and Hunter stood outside by his front gate. After he pecked her cheek, she bent down and scooted inside a taxi.

"Goodbye," she uttered from the window as the cab pulled away.

Hunter shook his head as he watched her for what was likely the last time. Once the cab vanished from sight, and he tugged his attention away from that direction, he noticed something interesting across the street. Giselle had observed him. She also watered her lawn while looking downright evil. Hoping to lighten her mood, he greeted her with a smile and a good morning.

Giselle didn't answer. In fact, she rolled her eyes at him and continued aiming her hose at the grass. Knowing he better get away before she aimed it at him, Hunter hurried into his house mumbling, "Women. Women are driving me crazy."

Sunshine blazed through the blinds of the ICU room where Serita rested. Her eyes fluttered open. She struggled to adjust her sight to the brightness. A nurse walking by the door noticed her waking and Serita noticed her, too. A short time after, Serita saw the nurse enter her room with a doctor.

"Mrs. Johnson, I'm Dr. Hayward." Lightly he touched her face and shined what looked like a miniature flashlight in her eyes. "You're back and we're very glad to see that. Very glad."

"Back?" Serita said weakly. "What…?"

"You've had surgery," he stated in a subdued voice.

"Oh, my God." Tears formed in her eyes. "What happened? I can't remember."

Dr. Hayward's chubby hand patted hers.

"Don't worry. It's common for a person to experience memory loss after a severe head injury.
Usually the individual won't remember the
events right before the trauma. We're just so
grateful you're back with us."

"Head injury?" Serita mumbled, looking
confused. "What…?"

The next day, Serita sat in bed one hundred
percent alert, but with her heart once again broken
from grief. When she asked about Chris and the
doctor reluctantly told her about his death, she
had been inconsolable. Now, many hours later,
Serita still felt dazed from the life-altering news.

Endlessly she wondered how life could be
this cruel to her and take away someone else
beautiful from her world. What horrible thing
had she done to deserve this? More importantly,
what had Chris done for someone to come in his
home and kill him?

As Mrs. McFee sat by Serita's bedside, she attempted to comfort her. The spirited, senior widow
had moved to the island within the last nine months
after living in Detroit for her entire life. After one
glorious summer spent on Madera Bay, Mrs.

McFee fell in love with it so much that she relocated there. Instantly Serita and her father became great friends with their next-door neighbor.

"Do you need anything, dear?"

Serita took a deep breath. "What I need I can't have anymore. But thank you for being here and looking after me. It means a lot."

"Someone else has been looking after you, too."

"Who?"

"That curly haired fellow that used to come by your house."

"Mitchell?" Serita said with surprise.

"Yes, I did hear people calling him Mitch."

"He's only been around because what happened was a police matter."

"Oh, no. It wasn't just that. He rode in the ambulance with you. And when I arrived, he was sitting at your bedside. He's sat with you for hours and hours. He wouldn't have left if someone hadn't called him away. I used to see him coming by your house before you married. You seemed to really enjoy each other."

"We did."

"So what happened?"

"I…I found out that he was married."

"Oh, no." Mrs. McFee clutched her sunken cheek.

"He's married to Julie Branson."

"Isn't that that rich girl? The one with the auburn hair?"

"Yes, that's her—her of all people. Even before the problem her family caused my mother, something told me not to trust Julie. I would see her at school and she would have this big, phony smile plastered on her face. Then I would catch her off guard, looking at me in this mean way. I also heard from friends that behind my back she called me half-breed because my mother was half Indian."

"Ah, she's just jealous."

"In school, she used to love to talk about her family's long history on the island. I guess that's why the Bransons act like they own it."

"They don't own anything."

"Aside from all that, Mrs. McFee, I swear I didn't know Mitchell was her husband. And I wasn't trying to get back at her for anything her family did to my mother. I just met someone who I thought was a good man, and who I thought was single, and I fell for him." She cast her eyes downward.

"We all make mistakes, dear." Mrs. McFee patted her hand. "We all do. The important thing is that you made it right once you found out about his situation."

Not long after Mrs. McFee had left to go home and feed her kitten, Mitchell strode into Serita's room, surprising her. His appearance also stirred up her rage.

"So did you find out who shot me and..." She blinked back tears. "Chris?"

Mitchell sat and pulled his chair close to her bed. "How are you feeling, Serita?"

"I guess I'm doing pretty good for someone who survived a bullet in the head." Bewildered by such a horror, she shook her head. "Why would someone do this? Was it for money? Was I robbed? Because we surely hadn't done anything to anyone."

"Before I can comment on any of those words, I just want to tell you that I'm so relieved that you're going to be all right."

"Thank you. I appreciate that."

"You were lucky."

"Yes, I am. *Blessed* is my word for it. The

doctor told me if the bullet penetrated any deeper, I would have suffered serious brain damage or even died."

"I'm so, so grateful that didn't happen." He gazed deeply in her eyes. "You have no idea."

"I'm grateful, too. Very, very grateful. But I want to know what you plan to do about this deranged killer. Did he take money? Is that why he did this to me and…" Chris's name choked in her throat.

Mitchell dropped his head.

"What is it?" she asked noticing his hesitancy in responding. "Why can't you tell me anything? You need to get that animal that did this!"

"I need to ask you some questions."

"But I can't remember anything. Everything is confusing. I was cooking French fries for Chris in my kitchen and now I'm here like this and he's…" She blinked back tears again.

"Did you and Chris argue about anything?"

Serita frowned at him. "What kind of question is that? What does that have to do with that cold-blooded killer you're looking for?"

"I don't have to look anywhere. We know who the murderer is."

Chapter 3

"Then who is it?"

"Chris. Chris did the shooting."

"What!" She clutched her chest to tame her racing heart. "You're nuts!"

"No, it's true. The evidence indicates that he shot you and then shot himself. We have the gun with his fingerprints on it. There isn't anything missing, so it wasn't a robbery. It was Chris."

"No!" Wildly Serita shook her head. "I can't believe you!"

"Serita, I hate to tell you this, but it's true."

"No, you hated to see me happy! You're mad because I found out you were a cheating married man and kicked your butt to the curb! You just didn't want me to be happy with anyone else! That's what this is about!"

"That's not true. And I told you if it wasn't for the twins we're adopting, I would have left Julie. You know I love..." He hushed and looked away from her.

"If you were going to say you loved me, I won't fall for that anymore. Don't even try it. And please don't you ever say again that my husband shot me and killed himself."

"But it's the truth. And it hasn't been the first time he has done something criminal."

"What do you mean?"

"I mean I ran a check on Chris Johnson. I bet you didn't even know he did time in prison."

Serita's eyes nearly bulged from their sockets. "For what?"

"For robbery and attempted murder when he was in his early twenties."

"No," she said in a faded voice.

"Yes. Serita, you didn't even know this man. Three months wasn't enough time to know him."

* * *

In the days during Serita's recovery at home, she wallowed in a deep state of depression over Chris's passing. Mrs. McFee tried to cheer her up by baking her favorite dessert, peach cobbler, and frying her mouthwatering fried chicken. Her good friend Lauren also visited her a few times, bestowing on her lots of hugs, laughs and uplifting talks about bright days ahead. Serita appreciated the kind acts.

Even so, nothing alleviated her tortured feeling. Compounding her heartache was her inability to remember what happened. Just as frustrating, she hated what Mitchell believed about Chris—that he'd shot them. It also distressed her to learn that Chris had been imprisoned. Why hadn't he shared that with her? Didn't he say he'd shared everything with her?

Despite his small deceit, knowing Chris the way she did, the accusations of him trying to murder her and killing himself made no sense to Serita. If only she had known some family or even friends whom she could have talked to about Chris. However, she didn't know any of his friends, other than Lauren's husband. As for family, Chris's sole living relative was his grandfather. He resided in a nursing home stricken with Alzheimer's disease.

In spite of what Mitchell told her about Chris, she would never believe that he hurt her. In her heart, she knew Chris loved her as much as she loved him. Someone else had murdered Chris and attempted to murder her that night.

Because of that animal, she had installed an alarm system in her house. She also vowed that when she became financially able, she would hire a private investigator to probe into Chris's murder. Along with that, she wanted the PI to investigate another matter close to her heart.

Serita felt especially emotional about that matter close to her heart one day as she visited the island's floral shop. It was the first time she had stepped out of the house since Chris's memorial. For some reason, she expected folks to gawk at her or possibly treat her differently. Much the opposite, everyone extended their sympathy and condolences. That is, until, Victoria Branson and her daughter Julie drifted in the floral shop as Serita browsed around.

"I heard about what happened," Victoria said

before even uttering a hello. "Next time you'll be more careful." Her hard, overly powdered features formed a snobbish pout.

"Excuse me," Serita said looking as testy as she sounded.

Julie stepped forward tossing her auburn locks away from her face and smirking. "What my mother is saying is that you just can't fall over any man who winks his eye at you. You have to be selective. Otherwise you'll wind up with another maniac who'll try to take your life."

Red-hot rage surged through Serita from the insensitivity of these two snooty troublemakers and she could not contain what flew out of her mouth. "My husband was no maniac! He was murdered! Don't you two meddling witches have anything better to do with your time?"

"No reason to get so defensive," Julie said with a hint of laughter in her voice. "We really meant no harm."

"Yes, you did. Just like your mother harmed my mother with those nasty things she said years ago." Serita threw a glare at Victoria Branson's small, crinkled eyes. "You are just so miserable. It must be hell to wake up every day and be you!"

Having spoken her mind, Serita stormed out of the shop, hoping she never ran into those two again. She pitied Mitchell. He married into a horrible family.

However, just days later as she soaked in the sun at the highly populated section of Madera Bay's Beach, she saw another Branson treading toward her. Rod Branson had always behaved friendly toward her ever since she could remember, even after his father shattered her mother's life. For that matter, the Branson patriarch, Phillip, had also tried to be kind to Serita.

After she graduated high school with outstanding grades, Phillip Branson offered her a corporate job in his mega successful soda company on the island complete with an exorbitant salary. With it, the elder Branson extended Serita other generous gestures. Because of the havoc he wreaked on her mother's life, nevertheless, Serita always told him to go to hell. She had attempted to do the same to Rod. He ignored her hostility and always tried to befriend her anyway.

"It's so good to see you out," he said, taking a seat on her beach blanket. "How are you feeling?"

"I'm fine. Thanks for asking. How are you?"

"Much better seeing that you're doing well."

Serita looked into his deep-set eyes set on an angular face. On several occasions in the past, Rod had made it clear that he longed to be more than a friend. Yet due to their family history and her lack of attraction to Rod, Serita always declined. Though, she had decided she could at least be civil to him. After all, his father had wronged her, not him.

Rod had even expressed to her that he had no control over his father's actions, but wished he did. He claimed that he would make him recant what he had done to her mother. Serita believed him. Rumor had it that his father and he had a volatile relationship.

"I feel badly about your husband," Rod continued. "No one deserves to die that young and so brutally."

"I appreciate you saying that. But I suppose you believe what the police say about him doing the shooting."

Rod shook his bald head. "No, I don't. I believe you. I read all about it in the papers. And I read that you believe someone else did it. Can you remember anything?"

Serita peered out at the ocean. Dozens of swimmers enjoyed the water. Their images faded because of her thoughts. "I try. I really try to, but nothing comes."

"You'll remember one day. When you least expect it, it will dawn on you and you'll get that killer. I hope they give him the electric chair. Well, let me get back over to my friends." He stood and gazed down at her with smiling eyes. "You take it easy now."

"You, too."

In the months that followed, Serita concentrated on moving forward. She went about straightening her financial affairs so she could not only hire an investigator, but also start a new business. Since she had graduated college ten years ago, she had worked alongside her father in his small, accounting firm. The work bored her out of her mind. Nevertheless, she never had the heart to tell her father. He loved working with numbers. More than anything, she wanted to please him. Now, the time had come to please herself.

What she envisioned was her own company

called Beautiful Things. Through an online catalog, other outlets and stores, she wanted to sell the most beautiful handmade items imaginable. The collection included bathing suits and sundresses she had designed and sewed for the long, hot days on Madera Bay. She would also sell homemade pillows, curtains, bedspreads and other soft ornaments to beautify the home.

She had crafted such merchandise for herself and her family. People always complimented her unique creations and asked if she had any available for sale. Now, in this new technology age, Serita felt the time to be perfect for her to be an entrepreneur and sell the lovely goods.

By a year's time, the following summer, Serita had designed and created enough items to start her business. Just as she prepared to take on the financial challenges of her venture, she received an exciting call from Lauren. Lauren and her husband, two teachers, had made a fortune creating some unique and sharp educational products for children. Schools, stores and other sources across the globe had taken substantial orders with them bestowing them instant wealth.

Because of this miracle, they wanted to

treat their best friends to an all expenses paid summer vacation to Nassau-Paradise Island in the Bahamas. Lauren, her hubby, an engaged couple, a young lady she met at Lauren's wedding and her husband's friend named Hunter were all invited to come.

Serita congratulated Lauren on her magnificent blessing. She also knew that the dreamy summer vacation sounded too exciting to pass up. She had never visited the Caribbean island and God knows she needed a lift. She had thought that by working on her creations, keeping herself occupied would lessen her sadness about her dad and Chris.

It did not happen. As the days grew, Serita felt weighed down with indescribable aloneness and emptiness. This trip was exactly what she needed. She couldn't wait to board the plane, meet Lauren and Damien's friends, and relax in that tropical paradise.

In Lakeside Virginia, Hunter enjoyed the last of a mouthwatering steak dinner served to him at his brothers' restaurant. Two of his younger siblings, Tyler and Dustin had created an eatery so popular and serving such delectable cuisine, they had already opened up another restaurant in his brother, Randall's St. Thomas hotel, The Sea Breeze Inn.

In fact, the entire family had become partners in the successful enterprise, investing either labor or money. Since Hunter had so many other opportunities he dabbled in, he had simply written a check as an investor.

After finishing his meal in the booth that he shared with his brother, Tyler, on this evening, Hunter gazed around the establishment scoping out the ladies. The eatery attracted a large female clientele.

"Some honeys up in here tonight." He shook his head. "Umm, umm, umm."

"But you're about to meet your friends on that island," Tyler said with a grin. "You're probably going to meet lots of cuties there. Plus, aren't your friends bringing some single ladies along?"

"One is single, a widow I heard. The other one I'm not looking forward to seeing again."

"Why not?"

"She's someone I used to see and we had a bad falling out. I wish Damien and Lauren hadn't invited her."

Tyler's warm brown eyes glistened. "Well, it's their trip and they're paying, so they can invite who they want."

"Actually, I insisted on paying for myself," Hunter said.

"So this cutie who you don't want to see, what happened?"

"None of your beeswax," Hunter said playfully.

Tyler laughed. "Must have been one of the crazy ones."

"I'm not talking about it."

"Because you probably acted like the player you are, and made her act up. Now you feel bad about how treated the lady."

"That's not true. I never mistreat women."

"You never give them a commitment when you know they want one. Man, why don't you just settle down?"

Hunter looked at his younger brother. "I don't see you settling down anywhere," he answered.

"That's because I haven't found the right lady yet. But when I do, I'm taking that big step. Look at those big, cheesy grins Jackson and Randall wear all the time."

Hunter eyed his two younger, married

brothers who sat across the room at a table. They appeared to have the time of their lives with their wives and children. "Yes, I guess those two are happy. They do wear goofy grins all the time." Hunter laughed.

Tyler laughed with him. "Keep playing. One of these days a woman is going to have you so whipped, you won't know what hit you."

"Never happen."

"It might be one of those you're going to meet up with at Nassau-Paradise Island. You've flown there lots of times. You know how romantic it can be. Strange things can happen in that atmosphere."

"Hey, I'm just going to have myself a good time and come back to my home—alone."

Just then, Hunter looked worried when he saw a heavyset, senior woman with short curls. She weaved through numerous restaurant tables, making long strides his way. Ever since his Aunt Essie May had announced at his brother's Randall's wedding that she saw him getting married in a vision, Hunter avoided her.

"Hunter," Aunt Essie May said, standing above the table with her hands propped on her hips. "Why haven't I seen you in a while?"

Hunter looked up at the six-foot woman. "Just been busy with work and other things. It's nice seeing you, Aunt Essie May."

"It's nice seeing my brother's oldest child, too. Sometimes I think you'll forget about me."

"I would never forget you," Hunter said with a smile.

"No, never," Tyler added.

"You shouldn't. I used to powder and diaper your bottoms. Your daddy would put the diapers on you kids so terrible if your mama wasn't around. I was the one that kept your drawers from falling off of you!"

Hunter peeped around to see if any of the women he checked out heard the embarrassing words. He spotted an attractive woman giggling and smiled at her awkwardly. Aunt Essie May talked loudly and cared less if it bothered anyone.

"So what about a woman, Hunter?" she inquired.

"What about one?" He took a sip of the soft drink he'd been nursing.

"Aren't you going away with some woman? Your parents said you're going away to some romantic island."

"I'm going to Nassau-Paradise Island in the Bahamas."

She glowed. "Oh, that's nice. You're flying one of your planes?"

"No, I'm taking a commercial flight with a group of friends."

"Well, I told you before what I seen in my visions. You're going to get married."

"No, I'm not, Aunt Essie May," he said with a laugh.

"Oh, yes you are, boy. Have you been seeing anyone special?"

"No." He took another swig of soda.

"Well, look for a surprise then. Your future mate is on her way. Now, let me go tell your brothers over there what I seen in my vision about them. More kids. Lots more."

With that, Aunt Essie May darted over to Jackson and Randall's table. Hunter's eyes followed her until he noticed Tyler looking at him and cracking up.

"What are you laughing at?"

"You. Mr. Player, player is getting married. Now, that's funny."

Hunter waved at him. "Get out of here."

"Aunt Essie May's visions always come true. You know that. She was right about Jackson and Randall. You're next, my brother." Tyler reared back in his seat, folding his arms. "Whoo, I can't wait to see this."

"Man, are you out of your mind? You will never, ever see me getting married. Don't even say such a thing. It makes my stomach upset."

Chapter 4

After a pleasant flight on Delta Airlines, Serita met up with Lauren and her teddy bear of a husband, Damien, right outside Nassau-Paradise Island's airport. As they stood, basking in the island's beauty and their other guests found their way to them. Serita saw Damien's buddy, Greg, and his fiancée, Toni, whom she'd met at Lauren's wedding.

Not long after, a slender, caramel-hued woman with long, dark blond locks sashayed toward them. Serita remembered her as Karrin from Lauren's bridal party. She was a secretary at the elementary school where Lauren taught. Then, last to arrive, Serita beheld a tall, muscular guy who already looked lusciously sun-tanned.

He had seductive, brown eyes, close-cropped, wavy hair and a smile brighter and hotter than the Nassau-Paradise Island sun. Serita couldn't resist staring at him as he spoke to everyone else who he knew. Yet each time he gazed her way, she cast her eyes in another direction. She didn't want to appear enamored with the man. After all, he was handsome enough to make any red-blooded, unattached woman with working hormones not only gawk, but feel extremely warm in places. Serita found him gorgeous and it made her feel strange. She hadn't paid a man any attention since Chris had passed away.

After he hugged and greeted the couples and granted Karrin a brief embrace, he stepped toward Serita.

"How are you doing?" he asked.

Serita's full lips curved into a soft smile. "I'm fine."

"I'm Hunter."

"I'm Serita."

He granted Serita an intense look. "That's an unusually beautiful name. It suits you."

"Thank you. Your name is nice and unusual, too."

"That's because I hunt what I want." Hunter joked, causing everyone in the group to chuckle except for Karrin.

"My buddy here is crazy," Damien teased. "I might as well expose his secret."

"Don't interrupt me, man," Hunter said with his gaze never leaving Serita's face. "I'm trying to be friendly. And I'm glad I came on this vacation already. I didn't know Lauren had such a nice friend."

To that, Serita's dark, cinnamon skin blushed and she noticed Lauren shaking her head full of dreadlocks.

"He's starting already," she declared, making everyone laugh except for Karrin. "Mr. Hunter Larimore is something else. You hear what I tell you."

"Yes, watch out for him," Damien added playfully.

Hunter waved his hand at them. "Aw, you two married old folks be quiet."

Serita laughed at all the lighthearted fun. The only strange moment happened when she glanced at Karrin. Standing to the side with a stern expression, she found nothing funny. From Hunter's brief greeting to her, they knew each other. Yet from the way she suddenly looked at Serita, she wondered if Hunter and Karrin were more than friends.

Riding to the villa that Lauren and Damien had rented for their guests and themselves, Serita gazed out the window enjoying the lush beauty of the tropical paradise. It reminded her of Madera Bay in many ways. Though there were differences. This island air had more of the sea-drenched scent to it than Madera Bay. What's more, the palm trees appeared more plentiful and taller. A mild breeze flowed through the atmosphere rather than sweltering heat. Added to the splendor, exotic, colorful plants and flowers bloomed everywhere on the island.

Once the taxi drove them to their Spanish Mediterranean-style villa, everyone hurried up the pathway like giddy and excited children. It not only looked large and beautiful, but it also had a pink, sandy beach beyond it that bordered a blue-green sea.

Inside, everyone loved the comfy, but luxurious digs, decorated with modern furnishings in hues of beige, white and tan. The traveling crew also went about claiming their rooms. After the two couples settled into their bedrooms, Karrin staked her claim in the largest room. Serita took a smaller one. So did Hunter.

Admiring her bedroom and its pastel, flower-patterned wallpaper, Serita realized that she had forgotten her luggage. Just as she made a step toward the door to get them, she saw Hunter toting them into her room. The sight of him caused flutters in her stomach.

"Thank you. You didn't have to do that."

"But I wanted to." Hunter peered around the room for a place to drop the suitcases. "Where do you want these?"

"There is fine." She pointed to the corner.

Hunter set the baggage where she indicated and then stepped closely in front of her. "So are you looking forward to this vacation?"

Serita inhaled something coconut on him that

smelled sexy and delicious. "Oh, yes. I've never been here before. What about you?"

"Yes, I'm looking forward to it. I've flown here lots of times. But it's always great to come back."

"So you vacationed here a lot?"

"Not really. I'm a pilot."

"Wow," Serita said looking impressed.

"I love planes. Fell in love with them when I was a kid."

"That's nice. I've never known anyone who could fly an airplane."

"I enjoy it I can just get up there and fly for hours. I have my own airplane."

"Wow. That's fantastic."

"So what do you do when you're not vacationing with Lauren and Damien?" He stuck his hands in his pants pocket and tilted his head aside. "You look like a model or an actress."

A gentle smile curved Serita's plump lips. "I'm not either of those. But I'm about to start a new business where models are needed."

"Really? What kind of business?"

Before Serita could answer, Damien and Greg burst in her room looking for Hunter. Under his humorous protest, they dragged him away to show him a basketball court in the backyard.

Serita hated the interruption. Then again, she knew it was best that they hauled him off. Charming as Hunter Larimore was, she needed to stay far away from him. It somehow seemed unfair to her beloved Chris. Also, Serita sensed there was something going on between Hunter and Karrin.

After coming in from the backyard, Hunter unpacked his luggage in his room. Soon after, Karrin joined him. He had to admit that with her pretty, hazel eyes, and slim, toned body, she looked like a piece of caramel candy. Yet he knew all too well that too much candy was bad for you. He refused to rekindle his affair with her.

Lauren had introduced them two and a half years ago. They dated, but he ended it. The woman had issues. She turned out to be someone that led a double life. He couldn't handle what she did and shunned getting mixed up in her drama again. Besides, something drew him to that luscious creature in the other room. He had heard about the ordeal she suffered and hoped to lift Serita's spirits.

"So how have you been?" Karrin asked. She twisted her finger around a long wisp of hair.

Hunter stopped packing and granted her his attention. "I'm good. And you?"

"You sure look good." She stepped closer to him. "Life must be treating you very well."

"It is. And now I plan to enjoy this vacation with my friends."

"Me, too. Maybe we can get a chance to spend some time together again and catch up."

"How is your family?" he asked, changing the subject.

"My family is all right. Most of them still get on my nerves. What about yours?"

"They're doing great." Hunter resumed unpacking and hoped that she would leave. When she stepped closer to him, he looked at her. "Do you want something?"

"Yes, I do want something." She flashed a dazzling smile, highlighted with vibrant, red lipstick. "I, uh, just wanted to tell you that the time I spent with you was the happiest of my life."

"Really," Hunter remarked, reflecting on that. "That's nice for you to say."

"I mean it. Now I'm going to go change. I really don't want to wear so much in this beautiful weather. It's nice to just flaunt your skin if it looks good." She eyed him with a sultry expression. "Don't you think so?"

"If that makes you feel good, do what you like," Hunter said indifferently.

Inside her room, Karrin Cameron felt anxious rather than happy as she searched through the dozens of the sexy outfits she'd packed. She had to find the perfect one to entice Hunter. She had to look hotter than any other woman that crossed his path. After all, she knew from their history how females threw themselves at him.

The instant Lauren informed her about the trip to the tropical paradise and said that Hunter had been invited Karrin knew she had to be there. The timing couldn't have been more perfect. School was out. She had the entire summer off. She could think of no better way to spend it than with the man she fell in love with a few years ago. They would have a second chance.

No one would get in the way. It sickened her

when Hunter flirted with Serita at the airport.
Well, if the young widow had gotten her hopes
up, too bad. What's more, she wouldn't let the
little show Hunter put on bother her. He was just
trying to make her jealous. He still clung to a bit
of bitterness because of what had happened
between them. But once she gave him a taste of
her between the sheets his bitterness would be
gone. He would remember the sweetness—the
sweetness of her that he couldn't get enough of.
Furthermore, she had something important to
share with him—something that would make
Hunter Larimore all hers.

Hours later, the seven vacationers enjoyed
themselves on the island's Cabbage Beach. They
played volleyball alongside turquoise waters.
They barbecued lobster, shrimps, ribs, chicken,
franks and hamburgers. From a restaurant
nearby the beach, they ordered salad, breads and
beverages to compliment the meats.

When Serita became exhausted and took a
break from the game to relax in the sand, she saw
Hunter walking her way to join her. All afternoon he had kept a conversation going with her.

Throughout it all, she felt those flutters again. How could she help it?

Out on the sun-drenched beach, he donned a pair of swim trunks that showed off every muscle he had. Serita's breath caught in her throat more than once as she secretly checked him out. Unfortunately, Serita wasn't the only enthralled with Hunter. Anytime Hunter engaged Serita in conversation, Karrin intruded and joined them. Moreover, Karrin always said something to insult Serita in a sly manner. It boggled Serita's mind because Karrin had acted so friendly toward her at Lauren's wedding. She guessed that a dreamy man like Hunter Larimore brought out the claws in some women. When she had a chance, she planned to ask Lauren the scoop on Hunter and Karrin.

"So what are you doing over here all by yourself?" Hunter asked, sitting down in the powdery sand beside her.

"I'm just worn out from all the fun."

"You're having a good time?"

"The best." She watched a young girl surfing the ocean waves.

"Good, because a few times I looked at you and you looked sort of down."

Serita was stunned at his perceptiveness. Her mind had wandered to Chris often while playing the game and especially during eating. He loved barbecue. It just didn't seem right that she should be out on a lush, tropical island enjoying herself while he couldn't enjoy anything in this world anymore.

"I was thinking about something sad," she admitted, "but I'm fine now."

"Good."

Serita gazed out at the others playing volleyball. Toni and Lauren were losing to Greg and Damien. While she shook her head at her losing team, she sensed Hunter's eyes roaming over her body. He had done that during the entire afternoon, sneaking looks that she caught. Each time she busted him, he looked away embarrassed. However, this time when she met his gaze, he admired her openly.

"I hope you don't mind my staring, but that is one beautiful bathing suit you're wearing."

Serita looked down at the orange bikini she had designed. "You like it?"

"Oh, yes," he said and then gazed in her eyes. "You have the body for it."

Serita cleared her throat, trying to ignore the butterflies in her stomach. "I made this."

"You did?"

Serita told him about the business she planned to start and the items she designed. While she talked, Karrin strode over and parked her buns in the sand next to them.

"What are you'll talking about?"

"A business I'm starting," Serita answered.

"Serita designed the bikini she is wearing," Hunter said. "Isn't it awesome?"

Karrin's red, glossed lips formed a plastered smile. "I've seen those in stores before. Maybe you should do something to make it look a little different." She glanced down at the skimpy, fuchsia bikini she wore, and then eyed Hunter seductively. "Men can't take their eyes off me in this one I have on."

"Because it's so pretty," Serita complimented her. "The color looks good on you."

Karrin glowed and looked down, inspecting herself. "Doesn't it though?" Then she gazed up at Serita. "But as for you, I don't think a business selling bathing suits is going to really get the bills paid. Girlfriend, you might starve depending on that."

"But I'm not just going to be selling bathing suits. I sell summer dresses, skirts and tops. And I also have items for the home, such as bedspreads, curtains, pillows and these unique, soft handcrafted ornaments for decorating. I gave some to Lauren for her living room."

Karrin mashed up her face as if something tasted sour. "I still say that it sounds like a loser to me."

"Do you have any personal experience with this type of business?" Hunter inquired.

"No."

"Have you ever started any kind of business?" he inquired further.

"No."

"Then how can you tell her that she won't succeed?"

"I'm just saying that it doesn't sound like a sensible, moneymaking business idea."

"That's because it isn't your idea," Hunter pointed out. "Serita has a vision, and the creativity and the hunger to make it, and that's all she needs."

To that, Karrin threw her hazel eyes heavenward.

Yet Serita's gaze clung to Hunter and his to
her. He had expressed just what she felt about
her dream. Armed with her passionate vision,
creativity and hunger, she knew that somehow
she would make it happen. Moreover, what he
had expressed seemed as if he had peeked inside
of her soul and spirit. It amazed her.

On and on the conversation went with Serita
and Hunter discussing her enterprise and his
offering business knowledge about it. When
Karrin lured him away, informing him that she
needed to tell him something important in private,
Serita had to admit that once again she hated to
see him go. She enjoyed talking to him. He was
warm and intelligent, and he was like a shining
sun in her life after a hundred days of rain.

When Lauren became too pooped to play any
more volleyball, she flopped down in the sand
next to Serita.

"I saw you talking to Hunter."

"I was picking his brain about starting my
business."

"And you picked from the right brain. That

man knows how to make money. And I know what I'm talking about. He helped Damien and me with our new venture."

"He did?"

"And didn't ask for a dime when we cleaned up."

"Wow, he's something," Serita observed.

"He has all kinds of things going on, too. His private airline is just one of them."

"Yes, he was telling me about his businesses. He's real nice, too." She smiled.

"Yes, he is," Lauren agreed. "The brother has it going on. The only thing he doesn't have together is his love life."

"That's what I wanted to ask you about. What's the story with him and Karrin? Are they seeing each other?"

Lauren smiled, revealing an adorable front gap-tooth. "My, my now, is Ms. Serita interested in someone?"

"No," Serita said, toning down her excitement. "I was just curious. You know I'm still grieving over Chris."

Lauren sighed. "I know you miss him. You should miss him. He was a wonderful man who swept you off your feet and loved you. And you loved him just as much. But you have to keep on living, girl."

"I know. But…but it just doesn't feel right for me to just get out here and even try to get close with someone else when he's only been dead a year. Plus, I haven't even been able to do anything about what happened to him, or me, and it gets to me. It makes me feel like I have such unfinished business. Somebody killed my husband and the police don't even believe it. They're just letting a murderer walk around. If only I could remember." She rubbed across her forehead. "I ask myself everyday why would anyone want to shoot me and Chris? I just don't get it."

Lauren clutched Serita's hand. "Things are going to work out. Chris's killer and the animal that shot you will be found. Someone that does such evil is going to slip up and get caught. But in the meantime, Chris wouldn't want you to sit around crying over him. He would want you to have love. And you will. I know that bright days are ahead for you."

"You always say that."

"And it's true. And as for Karrin and Hunter,

they used to date a few years ago. I introduced them. But I don't know what's happening since we've been here with them. But I do know that Mr. Hunter can't keep his eyes off someone else." Lauren eyed her with a smile.

Hunter barely heard Karrin as she prattled about various subjects, ranging from how much she couldn't stand her siblings, to how many designer handbags she owned. As Karrin spoke Hunter's mind drifted to Serita.

His mind lingered on exotic, brown eyes, which stared into his as if he was every bit the dream that she looked like to him. He envisioned her long, wavy hair that blew in the island breeze so sensuously that he wondered how it would look wild and tangled on his pillow. He tried to imagine her body that was so sexy that it seemed as if was carved out of his most erotic fantasy— a body hugged in an orange bikini that made him lust so much that he still felt aroused nearly an hour later. He wanted to caress deep brown skin that appeared as if silk oil had poured over it, making him wonder how it would feel beneath his lips and fingertips. When he talked with her and he'd felt such a connection with her that it frustrated him when Karrin insisted she had something important to tell him. Now, Karrin and he had returned to the villa and she still hadn't revealed anything significant.

"So what is it?" Hunter asked as he opened his bedroom door. "What did you just have to tell me that is so important? Is my room private enough to tell me?"

Still clad in her bikini, Karrin sashayed inside the room and sat on the side of Hunter's bed. "This is fine."

Hunter leaned back on the wall with his arms folded. "So tell me."

She patted a spot next to her. "Come sit."

"I'm fine standing here."

With her lips curled flirtatiously, Karrin crossed her legs. "Scared you might not be able to keep your hands off me?"

"Karrin," he stated irritably. "Let's stop wasting time."

She frowned. "You're so different. I don't even know if I should tell you."

"I'm not different."

"You're different with me. You used to love

to laugh and play with me. You couldn't keep your hands off me. Now you're just so impatient with me."

Hunter sighed and shook his head. "Do you know how much you hurt me?"

"You hurt me, too."

"Do you know how I felt that night? There I am with my buddies. We're taking my friend to that gentlemen's club for his bachelor party, and who do I see there but you. Not only were you butt naked, but you were spread out over two guys and each of them had their hands all over you."

Karrin hopped up from the bed and moved toward him. "Hunter, I'm so sorry. Really, really sorry."

"Yes, I am, too, for being such a sucker."

"But you wouldn't make any commitments to me. You wouldn't even say you loved me. And I needed to take care of myself. The secretarial job at the school didn't pay enough."

"Karrin, we were seeing each other. If you needed something, you know you could have asked me and I would have given it to you."

"I didn't know anything. I told you that I

loved you over and over. You would never say it back. I told you that I wanted to marry you. You wouldn't even consider it."

"So you strip to get back at me, letting strangers fondle the most intimate places on your body?"

"Hey, a woman on her own does what she has to do to survive. I don't do it anymore."

"I'm glad you came to your senses. You could get raped or killed like that."

"But I need to tell you why I stopped. It has to do with the something that I have to tell you that's important."

"I've been waiting."

She took a deep breath. "I was pregnant. I was pregnant with your baby. I found out about it after we broke up...but I lost our child."

Tense silence trailed her revelation. Hunter's face reflected a mixture of shock and anguish. His gaze scattered about the room as he pondered the words.

"I miscarried," Karrin continued, drawing his attention to her. Her eyes glazed with tears. "And I went through it all by myself. I knew you didn't want me anymore. So I had to go through that on my own." She sat back on the bed and cried into her palms.

Hunter stood reeling from the news. He could have denied the truth of it. However, he recalled during the time near the end of their relationship, she had suffered nausea. She had also gained some weight. The thought of her being pregnant crossed his mind then. He shook it off. He believed she would have told him if she were.

Hunter hurried to the bed and held Karrin within his arms. "I'm sorry I wasn't there for you. No woman should have to go through that alone. It was my responsibility, too. I'm so sorry."

She buried her face in his chest and sniffled. "I knew you hated me, so I didn't tell you."

"You could have told me. I didn't hate you." He rubbed her hair. "I don't hate anyone. Stop crying now. Please."

When Serita returned to the villa, she showered and threw on a tank top and jeans. Lauren, Damien, Toni and Greg had decided to go canoeing on a lake. Seeing all of them coupled up made her feel like a third wheel. It also made her lonely for Chris. It put her in the mood for a pity party. Why did everyone else have their soul mate while some monster had taken hers?

Realizing she had to stop torturing herself that way, Serita focused on something uplifting. Instantly Hunter came to mind. She craved to chat with him more about her business. They were in the midst of an interesting conversation when Karrin lured him off. Serita wondered if she really did have something crucial to tell him. The timing seemed strange.

Serita breezed down the hall, hoping that Hunter had returned to his room. She wanted to resume where they had left off on the beach. However, she noticed his door ajar. Not only that, but when she peeked within the crack, she beheld an interesting scene.

Hunter sat on the side of the bed with Karrin. Tenderly he embraced her and stroked her silken tresses. The lovers had reunited, she presumed. Cringing at the thought of them catching her spying, Serita rushed away. As she went, she tried not to feel like a fool.

After all, whom was she kidding? She had not only wanted to pick Hunter's brain about her business; she wanted to spend more time getting to know him. His mind intrigued her, but so did his body. Though, seeing that he was involved with someone else, Serita knew she had to settle for amusing herself with the island's wonders. Perhaps spending the summer in a tropical paradise could make her forget how alone she was.

Chapter 5

As dawn brightened the island sky the next morning, Hunter woke up feeling downhearted. Hearing that he had conceived and lost a child had troubled him so much that he barely slept. Equally disturbing, he couldn't stop thinking about Karrin enduring that agony alone. She had a strained relationship with her family, so he knew they had not been there for her.

Lame as it seemed to him, Hunter wrote her a generous check to cover the medical expenses. Though, he still hadn't figured out how to make up for his emotional abandonment even though he never knew she carried his child. He also wondered if his breaking up with her had caused the miscarriage. After all, he had been livid after witnessing her sleazy acts with those men.

He had never told her that he loved her, because he hadn't. Neither had he even considered getting married as she proposed. Even so, he cared about her and attempted to show it—at least in the beginning he did.

The more he came to know Karrin, however, the more he realized their incompatibility. He was goal oriented and her goals were only to look good and have a good time. They had little in common. She valued material things as if her life depended on it. Furthermore, her personality was too unpleasant to take every day. He had never met a more negative person.

She complained and criticized anything, everything and anyone. Also, she argued a lot and loved an excess of male attention. That's why he didn't buy her story about stripping in the club because she needed money to survive. Karrin stripped for one reason and one reason only—she loved to see men go crazy over her face and body.

Refusing to let the situation get him down and intent to enjoy his vacation, Hunter switched his thoughts to another woman who made his heart feel lighter. Thinking of her, Hunter showered and dressed. Seconds later, he knocked at Serita's bedroom door. Perhaps if he showed her something on the computer in the room about her business, they could spend a little more time together and talk about other things. He really wanted to get to know her better.

As he stood in the hallway knocking, he saw Toni passing by. Wearing her standard no makeup look, and tiny Afro, she dressed in a pale yellow sweat suit that complemented her coppery skin tone.

Her high cheekbones balled up into little apples as she smiled at Hunter. "How are you doing today, sir?"

Hunter beamed, admiring how energetic she looked in the morning. "I'm very well. And you?"

"Never better. Just going to have myself a great time today."

"Me, too."

"Well, if you were looking for Serita, you'll have to find her on the beach behind the villa.

She woke early this morning and tried to get Lauren and I to go jogging with her, but we were too lazy and hungover from last night."

As Serita ran along the beach inhaling the sea air, it surprised her to see Hunter trotting her way. Conflicting emotions tugged at her at the sight of him. On one hand, she loved his company and wanted to become better acquainted with him. On the other, she debated whether to be around him since he'd clearly rekindled his relationship with Karrin. Then again, she acknowledged that talking as friends was harmless.

"Hey there," he said, jogging up next to her.

"Hey yourself." She ran at a breathable pace. "What are you doing out here?"

"I'm looking for you. Thought we would talk some more about your business and get some breakfast. I'd like to offer my expertise on websites, marketing and business plans."

For a second, Serita questioned why he wanted to dine with someone other than his girl-friend for breakfast. Perhaps Karrin liked to sleep late, she reasoned. What's more, perhaps Hunter simply enjoyed helping others get their businesses up and running after being blessed with so much success. He had certainly helped Lauren and Damien.

"Sounds good to me," she said. "I need all the help I can get."

They jogged farther on the beach. Hunter shared some problems he had in starting his businesses. Afterward he advised her on what she needed to do to get Beautiful Things up and running. By the time they dined at a cozy, beach-side coffee shop, they discovered they were both big dreamers. Hunter shared all kinds of dreams he wanted to undertake in the future. Serita shared the same, some of which she had never shared with anyone before—not even Chris. Hunter made her feel that comfortable.

"Wow," Serita gushed, gazing into his seductive, brown eyes. "I love the way you think. It seems like nothing is impossible to you. You make me feel like that nothing is impossible for me either by just sitting here talking to you."

"Anything is possible for you. And I'm glad you feel that way. I feel the same talking to you. I like the way you think, too, Serita. Sometimes I can't talk to other people about all the things I want to do. They would think my ideas are too out there."

"No, your dreams aren't out there. I believe you'll do everything you said you want to do. Look at the wonderful things you've done with your life this far."

"Well, from now on we'll talk to each other about our wildest dreams," Hunter said, staring in her eyes.

Serita gazed back at him and swore she saw something sensual in his gaze. Though she attributed it to her overactive imagination. He belonged to someone else.

After they left the restaurant, Serita and Hunter strolled along the beach en route to the villa. All the while, Hunter captivated Serita with tales about his travels around the world as an airline pilot. When Karrin spotted them on the beach, she practically stomped in their direction.

"Hey, Karrin," Serita greeted her with a smile.

Karrin parted her lips as if it were an arduous chore and replied dryly, "Hi."

"Good morning," Hunter also greeted her.

Karrin took a deep breath. "Good morning. But where were you?

Hunter's brows arched. "I was jogging and had breakfast with Serita. Why?"

"Because I was looking for you."

"What's up?"

"I needed to talk to you."

"About what?"

She sighed with aggravation. "About what we talked about last night."

"I see."

"Could we talk now?"

Hunter hesitated for a moment. "All right." He turned to Serita. "I hope I see you later. Lauren and Damien want us all to go out and do some fun things together."

"It sounds good to me," Serita said and saw Karrin throw her a peculiar look.

Soon Serita watched Hunter stroll off with Karrin and she missed him already. Getting to know him had felt heavenly and again she felt such disappointment that Karrin had taken him away from her. Then again, she had no rights to the man. Pondering what she could she do to quell her growing attraction to Hunter, Serita shed her exercise gear to reveal a hot pink bikini. She plunked down in the sand and faced the sea. She had only sat there a few seconds when a good-looking guy strode over with his dog.

In Madera Bay, Mitchell walked inside his mid-sized home and removed his tie. He yearned to get comfortable after a long day at work. Julie had hated the house when she first laid eyes on it and tried to encourage him to live in her family's mansion. Mitchell refused. Although he liked her father well enough, living with her mother and brother would have stressed him. What's more, he simply craved the comfort of his own space.

Kicking back on the couch, he wondered if Julie lounged about in another part of the house or remained at the hospital. Her father, who suffered with cancer, became gravely ill recently after not having any problems for a year. In any case, whether she was there or not, Mitchell rolled his head back on the sofa cushions, grateful for the solitude. The twins who had blessed his life this year were away at summer camp. He missed them, but the quiet felt good tonight.

At work, he still toiled away on the old case involving Serita. It had him spinning in a circle, which tired and frustrated him. Some days he even wondered if police work still mattered to him.

He had come to the island nearly three years earlier with Julie from Chicago. Back there, he was an officer with the Chicago police department. Julie had worked as a criminal psychologist. Their department often consulted with her.

Immediately Mitchell was attracted to her good looks and exciting personality. When they started dating, he saw more qualities in her that appealed to him. They married and lived contently for six years.

Her father became stricken with cancer shortly after Mitchell shot a teenager who had tried to shoot him in a botched robbery. After the kid died, Mitchell couldn't stop seeing the youth's face. Nightmares about the killing haunted him so much that he knew he needed a change from the fast paced, perilous life of a city cop. Julie comforted him. As well, he comforted her about her father. When she decided to return to her South Carolina birthplace, Madera Bay, he looked into joining the police force there.

Madera Bay turned out to be the most beautiful place Mitchell ever visited. The air smelled country fresh. Swaying palm trees greeted him every day as well as a blue-green ocean that always beckoned his body to its scenic waters.

That being as it may, it didn't take long for Mitchell to recognize that he had made a mistake—not in moving to the island with Julie, but in marrying her. Reunited with her wealthy family, she showed him a different side. She became preoccupied with status and appearances.

Her brother, Rod, greatly influenced her, luring her attention to the family fortune and her father's numerous businesses. Together they focused on giving the employees of his father's various corporations as little as they could get away with. Added to it all, Julie nagged Mitchell about giving up police work for the more lucrative corporate life in one of her father's companies. Determined to be his own man, Mitchell always declined.

Still, he tried to make a go of the marriage. Julie constantly brought up renewing their wedding vows. They even decided to adopt children since Julie appeared to be unable to

conceive. Hence, they went about the proce-
dures of adoption. It all made Mitchell believe
their marriage would feel right again.

Then came the day Serita Jones walked into
the police station. She wanted information on a
cold case—a case about her missing mother.
Mitchell delved into it despite the other officers
in the station telling him not to bother. They
claimed that Serita had hounded them about her
mother since she had been a teenager and needed
to give it up. After all, they couldn't fathom why
she would want to find her anyway. Not only had
Evangeline Jones abandoned her daughter, but
she was also at the center of the biggest scandal
to ever hit the island.

Mitchell probed into the case further. Appre-
ciating his help, Serita assisted him with any information he needed about her mother. They grew
close. They grew so close that he shunned his
marriage vows—shunned telling Serita that he
had taken them with one of her fellow islanders.

At that point, Serita and he fell in love and
became passionate lovers. He knew he needed
to tell her about Julie. He longed to tell Julie it
was over but he didn't. Serita discovered his

adultery on her own after she attended an island festival and Julie introduced her to her husband. More than anything, Mitchell still wanted to leave Julie for Serita. But by then, the adoption of the twins had come through.

He couldn't abandon innocent children, especially two who had already been abandoned by their parents. And no way could he let Julie raise his children on her own—especially since she was totally under the influence of her overly ambitious brother, Rod, and affected by her mother's feeling of superiority. He cringed at the thought of his children reared in an environment where money was valued over character. Scars of his own childhood still haunted him. His father had not lived in the household to offer guidance to his children, and Mitchell believed it had led to his brother's life of crime.

Contemplating all this, he saw Julie padding down the stairs.

"Oh, you're home," she said.

Mitchell sat up on the couch. "Yes, I got in a while ago. You went to see your dad at the hospital today?"

She nodded somberly. "He's not doing well. He's doing poorly actually."

"Sorry to hear that. I hope he gets better."

"He has to." Julie forced a cheerful expression. "Just think, a year ago he was on his way out then, too, and he came back. I'm praying that he'll do the same this time."

As Mitchell pondered that, he saw her mother amble inside the house from the patio.

"Hello, Victoria," Mitchell addressed her. "I didn't know you were here, too."

"Mitchell," she said with a nod. "And I am certainly glad to see you, but I have a bone to pick with you."

"Mother." Julie eyed her with a scowl.

"No, it's all right," Mitchell insisted, granting his mother-in-law his full attention. "What is it that you want to get off your chest?"

"It's about the disgusting thing that is going on on this island."

"And what's that?"

"The lack of a dress code."

"Dress code?"

"Yes, this island seriously needs one. The decent people that live here want one. And you must talk to the police chief about imposing a fine or even jail time on these young women for what they are doing this island."

"What are young women doing?"

"Walking around here half dressed like tramps."

Mitchell grinned, revealing a boyish smile. "Are you kidding?"

Victoria's harsh features became harsher. "Do I look like I'm kidding? It's just not proper for them to walk around here half naked in those flimsy see-through clothes, and have their breasts hanging out in low cut blouses, and wearing those short skirts. And when they do wear a proper length dress, it's just too tight."

"Victoria, this is a free country," Mitchell informed her. "Plus, those women aren't bothering you."

"It is a bother to see all that flesh. Decent people do not want that around them. This island will turn into a whorehouse."

Mitchell looked tickled at her exaggeration. "The police can't tell people what to wear."

"There are some that do tend to dress like sluts in this town," Julie added.

Mitchell gawked at his wife. "Not you, too?"

"Yes, me, too. I am offended by the tacky way these women dress. All they are trying to do is lure some woman's husband."

"They remind me of that Evangeline Jones," Victoria ranted on.

Mitchell's eyes narrowed and he looked intrigued. "How so?"

"She used to wear all these tight clothes to show off her figure and entice the men."

Mitchell grinned and rubbed his chin. "From the photos I've seen of Evangeline Jones, she didn't have to do much to entice men. The woman was extremely beautiful."

"She was not!" Victoria yelled. "Any piece of trash can smear their face with paint to lure a man. Real beauty doesn't have to be so flashy."

"I agree," Julie said. "And that Serita is just like her. She looks like her and acts like her, too. And look what happened. She marries a man in three months and he tries to kill her. Well, she asked for it!" With those words, she gazed at Mitchell strangely.

Beholding his wife's peculiar stare and hearing her mean-spiritedness, Mitchell wondered if she knew about Serita and him. He also studied her behavior in general, and her mother's tirade. The two of them had such hostility against Serita. Why did they hate Serita so much?

Chapter 6

Over the next week, Serita and the crew entertained themselves with all sorts of fun activities and adventures. They toured on a catamaran cruise. They indulged in an island safari. They explored the island in a helicopter. They gambled at the Atlantic, Paradise Island Casino. They delighted their taste buds at island restaurants. They shopped at the boutiques, stores and markets on the famous Bay Street.

Above all though, Serita had the most fun when Hunter chartered a fishing boat. The seven of them took to the high seas ready to capture the night's dinner. Serita especially appreciated the trip because she had told Hunter earlier in the week that even though she grew up on a southern island, she lacked any fishing skill. Fish literally ran from her, she joked. On this trip, Hunter promised to teach her to be an expert fisherwoman.

As they rode further and further out to sea with the light wind brushing her face, Serita felt thrilled. Hunter had everything to do with her exhilaration. During the days that the group enjoyed the island's wonders, he stayed at her side and they came to know each other even more. With each second spent around him, Serita saw so much in him that she adored.

In fact, Hunter spent so much time getting to know her that she became certain that she misinterpreted what she witnessed in his bedroom between Karrin and him. Possibly, he consoled her about some traumatic event in her past.

After all, although polite to Karrin, Hunter acted as if he hardly liked her as a friend and never behaved like a boyfriend. He didn't engage Karrin in conversation. He merely responded whenever she talked to him. Neither did Hunter act affectionately to her in the slightest way. What's more, he always seemed to try to get Serita alone so they could interact.

Though their one-to-one chats never lasted long. Karrin always wound up tailing behind Hunter like a lost puppy, infringing on whatever conversation or activity they had going on. On the boat, it turned out to be no different. Once Hunter began baiting Serita's hook, Karrin joined the couple.

"When you finish with her, I need you to help me," Karrin told Hunter. "I hate worms."

"I hate them, too," Serita concurred, watching Hunter preparing her hook. Once he finished, he eased behind her, put his hand atop hers, and together they cast the line out in the ocean.

"How's that?" Hunter's deep voice rumbled lowly against Serita's ear. "You have a good grip?"

"It's perfect," Serita said, loving his firm hold on her hand. Altogether, his nearness, touch, scent and sexy voice incited those butterflies in her again.

"Now can you help me?" Karrin asked.

"Well, I promised to help Serita fish today. But I'm sure Damien can help you. He's great at fishing and he won't mind giving you pointers. Why don't you ask him?"

Karrin huffed. "Because I want you to help me. You're the best."

"I'm not the best." Hunter glimpsed Damien. He laughed and talked with Lauren, Toni and Greg. "Damien is available. See." He threw his head in his buddy's direction.

Serita glanced aside and noticed how incensed Karrin looked. "You can help her, Hunter. I think I got the hang of it."

"No, I promised to help you catch fish and that's what we're going to do. Now, Karrin, I'm sure Damien won't mind helping you. He's very patient."

To that, Karrin sucked her tooth and stomped across the deck toward Greg instead of Damien. Immediately he began helping her bait her hook.

"Really, you could have helped her," Serita said, turning her head to look over her shoulder at Hunter's face.

Deeply he gazed in her eyes. "I want to help you. I like being here with you."

Their eyes lingered for a moment before Serita turned back toward the water. Those flutters in her stomach ran wild. Minutes later, she felt tugging at her line.

The excitement of it all made her bounce. "We have one! We have one!"

"Feels like a big one, too," Hunter added. "Now we're going to let the line down a bit more and let the fish get the taste and start eating. Then we're going to reel him in."

"Okay."

Serita did as Hunter instructed and soon they reeled in an enormous fish. Thrilled, Serita jumped with joy, and before she knew anything, she had her arms around Hunter in an embrace. He hugged her with equal enthusiasm. Matter of fact, he held her so long and so tightly, her butterflies grew to red-hot need in the bottom of her stomach. And when their faces swayed back as they embraced, Serita couldn't resist gazing at Hunter's lips just as he gazed at hers. In the heated moment, their faces even drew so close that Serita felt his breath on her cheeks. But realizing they were being observed, they moved apart.

"That's a good size fish," Lauren exclaimed as she walked over to them.

Damien trailed his wife. "It sure is. That's a big sucker there!"

Toni and Greg joined them and praised Serita's conquest. All the while, Hunter teased Serita about cooking the entire fish for him that evening. She teased him back that he better cook it himself if he wanted to eat it. The only person who refrained from commenting was Karrin. She stood at a distant section of the boat, her eyes burning into Serita. Serita didn't want her to feel left out, so she beckoned her to come over and join them. In response, Karrin seemed to seethe and remained where she stood.

Serita ignored her attitude and basked in the fun of the rest of the fishing trip. With Hunter's assistance, she caught several more fish. Each time they had a catch, Serita couldn't resist hugging him. During those moments, he clung to her as if he hated to let her go. Serita was reluctant to let go, too. It felt so good to hold Hunter and feel him hold her that at times she wondered if she dreamed these moments in paradise.

That night as Hunter and the crew had a fish fry in the villa's backyard, he couldn't keep his eyes off Serita. He had such a fabulous time with her during the week and especially during the day that he longed to spend some time alone with her. As they fished, and particularly when they held each other, excitement filled him that at times overwhelmed him. He felt like a teenager with a crush and overactive hormones.

The only unpleasant moments occurred when Karrin followed him like a shadow. At every second possible, she interrupted his conversations with Serita or just refused to let them be alone. In spending time with her and comforting her about the miscarriage, Hunter had tried to be kind and a gentleman. Yet he had begun to see that Karrin misunderstood his actions. She misinterpreted them even though he had extended nothing except friendship. Not once had he kissed her or touched her in an intimate way. Neither had he spoken anything to mislead her.

Tonight he decided that she wouldn't be there to interfere again. After everyone went to their rooms, he planned to visit Serita and see what those luscious lips tasted like. All day he had received the vibes from her that she wanted a taste of him, too.

Hours later, as everyone chilled out in their rooms, Hunter walked down the hallway toward Serita's bedroom. He had almost reached it when a familiar voice from behind called, "Hunter?"

Slowly Hunter turned and strived not to show his frustration. "Yes?"

"Where are you going?" Karrin asked. Flinging her long locks out of her face, she hurried to him.

Hunter took a deep breath. "Where are you going?"

"I asked you first."

"To…to Serita's room."

"Can I come?"

Puzzled at her, Hunter tilted his head. "Why? From what I've seen you don't talk to Serita that much. I mean unless I'm talking to her."

Karrin's lips curled into a vibrant smile. "Ah, don't say that. I'm trying to get to know her just like you."

"Well, I wanted to talk to her…talk alone."

"Can you talk to me…alone? I need to talk about what happened again."

"But we've talked about it over and over. I feel bad, Karrin. Really, I do. But it gets to a point that the sadness just wears you out. I'm worn out with it. For the rest of the vacation, I want to kick back and not talk about it. Neither of us can do anything about it. You need to move forward. We need to more on."

"I know, but I need you…I mean I just need to talk to you about it some more."

"I can't do it."

"So that's why you like talking to Serita so much. Because she doesn't wear you out with depressing talk?"

"I really don't want to get into this."

"Come with me for a walk on the beach? Let's get to know each other again." She clutched his hand. "I won't get all gloomy on you. I'll be fun like I used to be with you."

Hunter tucked her hand at her side. "Ask one of the others."

Karrin eased close to him and glided a long, red nail against his arm. "Come on now. Aren't you tired of playing buddy with me? I remember how you were, Hunter. I remember that drive of yours. You like beaches. You like doing naughty things in the sand." She eyed him seductively. "I can teach you some new, naughty things I know."

Quietly Hunter looked at her and realized what he had to do. Despite what happened, it served no purpose for them to hang around each other all the time. After all, she had now expressed she longed for more. He had to tell her they could only be friends.

But just then, he saw Damien strolling down the hall.

"What are you two up to?" he asked.

"We're about to take a walk," Karrin answered with laughter in her voice.

"No," Hunter said. "She's about to take a walk. I was on my way to see Serita in her room." He saw Karrin throw her eyes heavenward.

Damien scratched his head. "You got a problem then, buddy."

"Why is that?" Hunter asked.

"Serita is sitting out on the porch with some guy she met at the beach the other day. He has a puppy and they're playing with it." Damien said and continued up the hall to his room.

Hunter stood spinning with disappointment. Karrin touching his arm jolted him out of his haze.

"I guess she has company," she said, "so you can keep me company."

"Maybe someone else can walk with you. I'm going to my room to get some sleep."

Karrin sighed with frustration. "Fine then! Greg was in the living room watching television alone. I'll ask him. What do you think about that?"

"Go, do whatever makes you happy."

"I will!" Karrin flounced down the hall.

Hunter walked back to his room, feeling tempted to take a stroll out on the porch and check Serita's visitor out. Had she hooked up with someone on the island already? Then again, he had no right to behave like a jealous suitor. Yet this did make it clear what he needed to do. Now more than ever he had to make his move on Serita.

The next day as all the women pampered themselves at the spa, Hunter played basketball in the backyard with Damien and Greg. As all of them took a break and sat courtside, Damien and Greg expressed their observations about his love life.

"So what's up with you, man?" Greg asked. With a handkerchief, he swiped sweat off his slim face and looked at Hunter. "Which one are you with?"

Damien eyed Hunter curiously as well. "Yes, I'd like to know that myself. I see Karrin sticking to you like glue. But obviously, you're into Serita. You made your intentions quite clear on the boat." He wiped his chubby face with the back of his hand. "Man, I thought you were going to tongue her down right out there for everybody to see."

Hunter grinned. "I wanted to. I wanted to get all up on her."

Damien laughed lightly "You're too much, man."

"So she's the one you're tapping on this vacation?" Greg asked with a sly twist of his lips.

"No, I didn't say that," Hunter said. "But I want the lady to know I'm definitely feeling her."

"With the way you were acting on the boat everybody knows you're feeling her," Damien remarked.

"So what about Karrin?" Greg inquired.

Hunter waved his hand. "Oh, man, nothing is happening there."

"What do you mean nothing?" Damien pressed. "She has stuck to you like glue everywhere we went."

"I know and I'm tired of it."

Damien frowned. "So why are you putting up with it?"

"I can't really get into that. But believe me, we are not together in any kind of intimate relationship. We're just friends"

Greg smirked. "Because you want that fine Serita, right?"

Hunter's expression grew pensive. "Hey, she's gorgeous. But it's more than that. We can talk for hours and we just connect, and it's just something there. Something I can't describe."

Damien patted Hunter's shoulder. "Man, with the way you're talking and looking, you might break your rule."

"What rule?" Hunter asked.

"Your rule about falling in love."

"That rule will never be broken."

Damien smiled and shook his head. "Love doesn't take orders, my man, from you or anyone else. It jumps you—hard. Before you know it, it's there. Right, Greg?"

"That's your talk," Greg said. "I'm thinking about him not being with Karrin. That has me very interested." He rubbed his chin.

"What do you mean?" Hunter asked.

"Yes, what do you mean?" Damien added.

"It means someone has to take care of the beautiful lady's needs."

Hunter frowned at him. "Get out of here."

"I'm with you," Damien echoed his sentiments.

"No, I'm serious," Greg said smiling. "I might have to take care of that."

"And what about Toni?" Hunter blasted.

"What about her?"

"You're engaged," Damien reminded him.

"You two know me."

"And we thought your butt had straightened up when you met Toni," Hunter pointed out.

"Look who's talking."

"Hey, I'm straight with women," Hunter admitted.

Greg raised a wary brow. "Are you being straight with Karrin?"

"Look, there is a delicate matter and I have to be careful with her. But I haven't led her on at all. I never told her we are back together. I haven't been affectionate. I haven't kissed her. I've basically been a buddy."

"So would you mind if I tapped it?" Greg asked.

Hunter and Damien exchanged gazes and shook their heads.

"Aw, don't you two look at me like that. I love Toni and everything, but Karrin is fine. Superfine! And she has that look like she knows what to do between the sheets."

"So what?" Hunter shot.

"So she's giving me signals. Gave them to me the other night when we took a stroll on the beach. She just kept giving me the look and talking about how lonely she was."

"Because she was pissed at me," Hunter informed him.

Greg gave him a sidelong look of annoyance. "It had nothing to do with you! And I know that for sure because she's given me signals before. I've told Damien about them."

Damien sighed. "And I wish you hadn't."

"What?" Hunter scowled. "Something happen I don't know about?"

"Well…" Greg leaned toward them and lowered his voice as if disclosing a confidential secret. "One time her electricity wasn't working at her apartment and she stayed a week with Toni and me. And when she took a shower when Toni wasn't there, she left the door open."

"Maybe by accident," Hunter pointed out.

Grinning, Greg shook his head. "No, it wasn't an accident."

"How do you know?" Hunter asked.

"Because I peeked in and she smiled. Then she started giving me a show. Her body was beautiful—so, so beautiful. And she started rubbing soap over it all sensuously. I was like damn. Then I heard Toni come in the house downstairs, so I closed the door and got away from there. But I swear to you two, if Toni hadn't come home, I believe Karrin would have hit it."

"That's so foul," Hunter remarked.

"For real," Damien added. "And I told him that when he first told me about it."

"What's so foul about it? She wanted me. And if Hunter isn't going to step up to the plate, then I'm ready."

Hunter shook his head. "You're nasty, man. Toni is a nice lady. Don't do that to her."

"I'm with Hunter," Damien expressed. "Toni is the best thing that ever happened to you. Why mess that up?"

"And look at what Karrin is doing to Toni," Hunter went on. "What kind of woman does that to her friend?"

"A woman who is hot for a man," Greg boasted with a grin. "She can't help herself."

"No," Hunter countered, "a woman with problems. I'm going to tell you something about Karrin. When we were together, I had all kinds of issues with her personality that turned me off. But then I walked in this strip club one night for my buddy's bachelor party and there she is naked and with two guys' hands all over her, and that helped me make the decision to end it. Do you still think she is worth messing Toni over for?"

Greg thought for a moment and his lips curled mischievously. "Hey, she's fine. You'll know I'm a wolf. I have to taste that."

Hunter sighed. "I give up." He stood and bounced his ball back on the court.

"Me, too," Damien said, following him.

Karrin left the spa earlier than Lauren, Toni and Serita because she wanted to catch Hunter at the villa. She wanted to catch him alone and ravish him with what she had held back during their time on the island. She had played her innocent act to the hilt because she sensed his lingering resentment toward her and knew getting in his good graces again required work. Now, the time had come for her to stop pretending to be his friend and the ex lover that he comforted after a heartbreaking ordeal.

Yet when she arrived at the villa, Hunter wouldn't budge from his buddies and that basketball court regardless of how she tried to entice him away. She had even apologized for her rant the other night.

Hunter preferred to hang outside on the court. Much the opposite, Greg dropped by her room repeatedly. With his ordinary looks and lean frame, he looked nothing like her type. Still prior to the trip and before this opportunity of reuniting with Hunter, Karin had flirted with Greg. She became so bold with it that she titillated him with her birthday suit in the shower at Toni's house. She got a kick out of the lustful look on his face. It hardly mattered that Toni was a good friend. She never cared much for what women thought anyway. Men were what she lived for.

Ever since Toni started dated Greg a year ago, Karrin always noticed Greg staring at her face and body. He did it so much and so blatantly that he made her feel extremely desirable. That's why she ran to him the other night to make Hunter jealous—because he made her feel sexy and beautiful. If only she could incite such desire in Hunter, and have him drool at her the way Greg did.

Mystified at how to soften Hunter toward her, Karrin plopped down on her bed. The way Hunter treated her saddened her. Although he had behaved respectfully, he had not acted the slightest bit loving toward her—even after she told him about the miscarriage. She had counted on that bombshell to draw them closer. It hadn't. For some reason that she couldn't figure out, he seemed to be obsessed with hanging around Serita. Equally irritating, Karrin hadn't missed the way Serita acted around him.

It broke her heart when she witnessed their antics on the fishing boat. She had not only had to deal with Hunter's eyes devouring Serita, practically undressing her, but with Serita doing the same to him. Far worse, several times it appeared as if Hunter wanted to kiss Serita and as if she longed to kiss him in return.

Rehashing it all in her mind caused Karrin to get up from the bed. Unable to contain her rising frustration, she paced. All week Hunter had paid more attention to Serita than he did to her. All week she had stood by as they talked nonstop and made her feel like an intruder. All week she had wanted to scream and smack Serita. She had no business having an attraction to Hunter anyway. Her husband had just passed away. Lauren had told her the story. She deserved Hunter, not Serita. Serita had loved her dream man and married him. And now she wanted to love Hunter.

Hunter Larimore had touched a place in her heart ever since she met him. God knows she had met a lot of men, but none affected her the way he did. Not only was he the handsomest and sexiest looking man she ever met, but in the bedroom he remained unmatched. The things he did to her body that drove her wild Karrin couldn't even describe. All she knew was that she ached to feel such a high degree of passion again.

Yet there was more to her captivation with Hunter. He was extremely intelligent, ambi-

tious, fun and so down to earth. Even when he
met her family who often embarrassed her with
their lack of sophistication and tactlessness,
Hunter fit right in.

In no time, she fell in love with him and confessed her feelings. Every day she hoped that
Hunter would feel the same and express the
same. She gave him the hottest love she could
and always made sure she looked ultra gorgeous.
Still, he refused to utter those magical words
that she hoped would open the door to being
Mrs. Hunter Larimore. Neither would he even
consider marriage. By then she felt herself losing
her grip on him. Somehow, he had drifted away.

The strip club came about because of her re-
taliation against Hunter and a means to make tons
of money. On top of it all, she knew how beautiful she was and loved men drooling over her. It
turned her on. Though, she would have given it up
to make one man drool at her forever—Hunter
Larimore. But after he caught her at the club, he
ended their relationship. A month later, she
learned of her pregnancy when she miscarried.

Karrin flitted over to the mirror and gazed at
herself with a devious smile. She had tired of

withholding all the loving she ached to lavish on Hunter. Serita was no match for her in any way. Now, she had to take out the heavy artillery. Tonight she would seduce Hunter. With his sex drive, their chemistry and her hot looks, there was no way could he resist her—not even for Serita.

Miles away, while Toni received a facial at the spa, Serita and Lauren took a stroll around the posh, hi-tech facility.

"Guess what I found out from Damien when he called me a few minutes ago?" Lauren said.

"What?"

"Hunter is not with Karrin. They're just friends."

Delight brightened Serita's face. "I'm so glad you said that. Because that's what I suspected. He doesn't act like her boyfriend. But why is she following him around like a shadow? I know she's your friend, Lauren, but he can't make two steps without her."

"Well, he told Damien and Greg that something happened that he can't share, but he's basically being a friend and supportive to her. But he's definitely into you."

Serita's face lit up even more. "Really? Because he is the first man since Chris that has me…"

Lauren looked at her curiously "Has you what?"

"I don't know." Serita shrugged. "I guess he makes me feel like a woman again. The other day on the boat, everything he did just drove me crazy. I thought about him all night."

Lauren chuckled. "That's wonderful. And I saw you two. Thought you were going to kiss several times."

"So did I. That's when I really knew he couldn't be with Karrin. He couldn't disrespect her like that. He's not that type of man. They had to be just friends."

"So what are you going to do about it, missy?"

Serita glowed. "I'm going to get with him. I mean get with him alone so we can get to know each other better."

"When?"

"Tonight."

Inside his room, Hunter had heard Serita, Toni and Lauren in the hallway. As they laughed and talked, he assumed they had just returned from the spa. After giving Serita fifteen minutes to settle down, he opened his door in hopes that they could spend some time together. As soon as he stepped into the hallway, Karrin appeared.

"I was just about to go out," he told her.

"Where?" she asked, easing close to him.

"Look, Karrin, we need to get something straight. I think of you as a friend and I can't spend all of my vacation time with you."

Karrin looked like a wounded puppy, but instantly her expression brightened. "You're just saying that."

"I'm not just saying it. I mean it."

"No, you don't. You have to be reminded of something. You have to be reminded of how good something was."

With that said, Karrin shocked Hunter by pressing her mouth against his. As Hunter pulled away and she slipped her arms around his broad shoulders, kissing him more ardently, over her shoulder he noticed someone was walking their way. He saw Serita walking in their direction.

Chapter 7

Hunter saw Serita's eyes nearly bulge out of their sockets at the sight of Karrin kissing him. Then, in a split second, she rushed away in the other direction. By then he had broken free from Karrin, but she attempted to get a second chance at a hot lip smack.

"Look, Karrin," he said, dividing his attention between her face and seeing Serita escape to the living room. "I really, really mean what I'm saying. We had a nice time together for a while a few years ago. And I'm truly sorry about what happened, but it's been long over. I have no feelings like that for you any longer. I don't want to lead you on."

The playful expression Karrin had worn grew hard and furious. "Because you want some new booty? Is that it?"

"Don't act like that."

"You don't tell me what to do."

"You're right. But I can tell you what I can do. And I choose not to get involved with you again. We have little in common and we're just not compatible."

"We're damn sure compatible in the bedroom."

"I want more."

Her face softened and suddenly she looked as vulnerable as she sounded. "I've changed. I don't strip anymore and I'm getting my head more together. I'm more mature and I think differently. I think like you do. About making big things happen. If you just give me a chance and get to know me again, you'll see we have everything in common."

"There's somebody out there for you. But it's not me. Have a nice evening."

Hunter strode down the hall in search of

Serita. He knew Karrin remained where they stood, probably throwing invisible daggers in his back. But he couldn't see himself wasting his time or hers. They just weren't right for each other. Something inside kept telling him that Serita was.

He hurried farther down the hall and then into the living room, where he had seen Serita flee. Damien, Greg, Toni and Lauren hung out on the sofas enjoying a comedy on cable.

"Anybody know where Serita went?"

Lauren threw her head full of dreadlocks to the front door. "I think she's on the porch."

"Thanks."

Outside on the veranda, Hunter saw Serita leaned back against the wall. With an uncomfortable expression, she glanced at him, and then gazed out at the darkness.

"I was looking for you," he said.

Her gaze stayed fixed in the distance. "Why?"

"What you saw was nothing."

"It's none of my business, Hunter."

"Oh, yes, it is."

"No, it's not. What you and Karrin do is not my business."

Hunter stepped in front of her, forcing her to look at him. "She kissed me and I pulled away. I told her that we can only be friends. That's what you saw. And if you don't believe me, I'll say it in front of her."

Serita stared at him in confusion. "I—I didn't mean to interrupt."

"There was nothing to interrupt."

"I was just going down the hall."

"To see me?"

She lowered her head. "Yes."

Gently he touched her chin, causing her to look up at him. "I was coming to see you, too. I feel something between us. Karrin and I used to date a few years ago, but it has long been over. I have feelings of friendship toward her. I just told her that."

"But you're always with her."

"Because she told me something that she went through when we broke up, something that I'm partially responsible for. And I felt obligated to give her emotional support. But she had other ideas. And I'm not about that with her. I feel something strong growing between you and I in this short time we've known each other. Don't you feel it, too?"

Serita nodded. "Yes, I do. I was coming to your room to see if we could spend some time alone."

"I wanted the same thing." He became quiet and gazed at her lips. They looked full and shimmered beneath the moonlight. "And I wanted to do this."

Hunter stepped close to Serita, cradled her face in his palms and brought his lips near hers. Although, just as they were about to kiss, the screen door swung open.

"Sorry you two," Damien said. "But, my man, someone has been trying to reach you and couldn't get you on your cell. He said it's urgent."

"Oh, my battery needs charging," Hunter said. "Who is it? Nothing can be that urgent." He gazed at Serita. "I'm busy. Very busy with something very important."

A shy grin spread across Damien's chubby face. "It's the company who is servicing one of your planes. They said they need to ask you something."

"Aw shucks." Hunter looked at Serita. "I'm going to have to take this call, but I want you to stay right here. Don't move. We have to pick up where we left off."

Serita smiled. "I'll be waiting here."

* * *

As Serita reclined against the wall, her mind replayed the moments she had just experienced with Hunter. Magic transpired between them and it excited her so much that it scurried from her head to her toes. Hunter swept her up in a feeling that she hadn't felt in a long time—sensually alive. And if this was God's present for all the suffering she had endured, she couldn't wait to unwrap it and receive it all. Being around Hunter or just thinking about him gave her such a high.

"I'm back," he said, rushing out of the screen door.

"Took care of your business?"

"Yes, I'm having one of my planes serviced and the mechanic needed to ask me some questions." He stood in front of her again.

"Wow."

"What's the wow for?"

"I know people who get their cars serviced, but I've never known anyone who had their plane serviced. You're just awesome." His eyes entranced her and she dropped her fascination to his lips.

"Oh, Serita," he said, his voice fading as he

stared at her mouth. "I want to be awesome to you."

Hunter stepped so close to Serita that their bodies pressed. Just then, though, the screen door opening and slamming drew them apart.

Awkwardly Karrin stood looking from face to face. "Hunter, I answered the phone. A guy is on the line and wants to talk to you about one of your planes. He said you just spoke to him."

"Damn!" Hunter said and gazed at Serita. "I'll make it short again."

She nodded. "All right."

Hunter dashed in the house. Karrin remained outside. Serita noticed her observing the stars and darkness, before she focused on her.

"So are you having fun on the trip?" Karrin asked.

"I'm enjoying it a lot," Serita answered, sensing her working up to something. "What about you?"

"Yes, I'm having the time of my life. All these men are after me. Matter of fact, even my ex is after me and I'm just trying to be friends with him."

Getting her drift, Serita stared out into the dark and hoped that Hunter would return soon. Even better, she wished Karrin would just go away.

"So I bet you miss your husband."

The remark drew a hint of a frown on Serita's face. "Excuse me?"

"I mean, I'm sorry about your loss. I heard that he passed away a short while ago."

"It was a year ago."

"Bet you miss him a lot. How long were you married?"

"Not long."

"And now you're back out here again."

"What do you mean back out here?"

"I mean that you're on vacation having a good time and trying to move forward. You're trying to forget your husband and get yourself a new man. That's sensible." She stared at Serita with a smug expression. "Besides, I guess it doesn't take long to get over someone."

Serita's throat tightened with too much emotion to respond. She pulled open the screen door and hurried to her room. After she plopped down on her bed, she realized she had been foolish to let Karrin steal her joy. She wanted to ignore her insinuation that she had hardly grieved over Chris before moving on to the next conquest, but a dark feeling welled up inside of her. It compelled her to reach for her purse, pull out her wallet and remove a wedding photo from it. Chris and she had taken it on the day they married. Tears soon distorted images before her eyes. Chris, she would never ever see him again.

Moments later, Serita drifted off to sleep. A knock on the door startled her awake. She sat up, recalled the somber feeling that enveloped her before she dozed off and then stepped across the room to look in the mirror. With a tissue, she blotted her tearstained face, and then opened the door.

Excitedly Hunter strode in until he really looked at her face. "What's the matter? Were you crying?"

"A little."

"What's wrong?"

"I don't want to get into it."

"I do, because if something is wrong, I want to help you make it right."

"You can't fix this, Hunter. You can't bring my husband back."

Hunter looked stumped.

"I don't know if Lauren and Damien told

you," she went on, "But my husband was killed last year, and I was shot."

"Yes, I did hear and I'm extremely sorry about him. But I'm so thankful that you're alive and well, and that I have been given this chance to meet you. You have no idea how thankful I am."

"And I'm so grateful to meet you, too. But..."

"But what?"

"Well, I...I was thinking about him after I left the porch, and I think it's better if I not get into any type of... Well...it's just too soon for me."

"What brought this on?"

"It doesn't matter."

"Did Karrin say something to you? I left you two alone."

"It's me, Hunter. My husband deserves more from me. He was a good man and I should grieve for him and not run into another man's arms so fast."

"Serita, from my understanding, it's been a year. That's not too soon."

"It is when you loved someone like I loved Chris. He deserves better. I haven't found the person that killed him. And I...I have to do that.

I just came on this vacation to give myself a spirit lift and I have it. I didn't come here to..."

"To meet me and feel something that reminds you of how alive you are." He stepped close to her. "Don't do this, to me or yourself, Serita. Let me get to know you and you know me. Let me kiss you." He slanted his face down to hers.

Serita gazed up at his handsome features. "Hunter, I'm tired. I'm going to shower and go to bed. Good night." She headed into her bathroom.

After Hunter stepped out of Serita's room, he hung his head and leaned back against the wall for a second. His mind replayed the discussion they'd just had. Then it recreated the moments on the porch. She was just about to let him taste those beautiful lips. What had happened during the time he left? He knew what happened, he suddenly realized. Angrily he strode down the hall and knocked on Karrin's door.

She glowed when she opened the door and saw him. "Hey? You came to keep me company? Come in."

"No, I don't want to come in or keep you

company. I want to know something. I want to know what you said to Serita outside."

"I didn't say anything to her—nothing except asking her about her husband. Lauren had told me about the situation. I offered my condolences."

Hunter's jaw tightened. "And why did you suddenly develop an interest in her husband?"

She shrugged. "Just making small talk."

"Why didn't you take your small talk in the house with the others?"

"'Cause I felt like standing outside and getting some fresh air. Darn, Hunter, I can't get some fresh air without you getting on my case."

"You wanted fresh air all right. You saw us getting close and you wanted to do something ugly to mess it up."

"I did not."

"Just stay out of my life, Karrin. Stay out of my life."

Far away in Madera Bay, Mitchell drove around the island after finishing his workday at the police station. A slow day, it had enabled him to review files in the Evangeline Jones case. He became so involved analyzing statements, documents and evidence, all pertaining to Serita's mother, that when he finished, he thought of a happier time in his life—the time with Serita.

As he drove, he couldn't help driving by her house. He was tempted to visit her house, but, he stopped himself. Being around her and especially in her house where they had shared so much passion, would have tortured him. He still hadn't gotten over how she made him feel.

Not a day went by when he didn't remember things she said to him and things he said to her. Not a day went by when he didn't behold her beautiful face and body in his mind. Not a day went by when he didn't close his eyes tight and recreate the hot love scenes between them that were like nothing he ever experienced.

He loved her. He loved Serita so much that when he arrived at his house and lay down with Julie, he knew the only way he could touch her was to imagine that she was Serita.

"Hard day," Julie said, easing behind him in bed, palming his broad back.

"Not that hard," Mitchell said, tensing as she touched him.

"Well, what about giving me some hard

loving?" She spoke in a teasing tone and coaxed him around by clutching his shoulders.

Mitchell turned around and faced her. He saw a beautiful woman—a woman that most men would love to have in their bed if they only went by her appearance. Yet with each day that he came to know Julie, it became harder to love her and make love to her.

Before long, she kissed him. He closed his eyes and kissed, too. And soon in his mind he lay on a carpet, his naked body entangled with Serita's. Fiercely he pounded her, making her scream and moan. He felt so turned on and breathless that he groaned with ecstasy. Yet swiftly the fantasy ended as he opened his eyes. Julie gave him her all, loving him passionately.

Chapter 8

The next day as Serita went for her morning run on the beach, she happened to see Hunter running, too. When he spotted her and jogged her way, at first she felt tension between them.

"Nice day for a run," he commented.

"Yes, it is."

Silence lingered between them and he cleared his throat. "Look, I'm sorry if I made you uncomfortable, Serita. I've never been married and lost someone that close to me, so I have no idea what it's like."

"No, you didn't make me uncomfortable. It's just me and things I have to work out."

"I didn't mean to pressure you."

"I didn't feel pressured, Hunter."

"Then is it okay if I still hang out with you today? I—I mean as a buddy. There won't be any pressure."

She smiled softly. "That's fine."

Their day filled up with golf, tennis and horseback riding, all with the complete group. All the while, Hunter stayed close by Serita's side, and they talked to each other more than they talked to anyone else. At times, for her it felt as if they were alone.

By late afternoon, the seven travelers finished a seafood feast at the Buena Vista restaurant. As Serita lounged in the afterglow of the tasty meal and exhilarating conversation, her spirit felt more uplifted than ever. Lauren had been right in predicting that joyful days awaited her. She almost felt like a different person. It had everything to do with spending time around Hunter. The only negative side was the dirty looks Karrin gave her all day.

At the wind up of the meal, Serita and Lauren wanted to shop and planned to meet up with the others later at the villa. Hence, they left the table and headed outside. Once beneath the vivid sunshine and away from Karrin, Serita couldn't help expressing her concerns.

"Lauren, Karrin has been giving me the meanest looks. Hunter says they are over, but she still must have deep feelings for him."

"Yes, I can see how jealous she is. But she's wild. She'll forget all about him when the right man comes up in her face."

Serita frowned at Lauren's tone. It seemed odd for her to speak so negatively about her friends. In fact, she had gotten the vibe the entire trip that Karrin had done something to irritate Lauren. "You sound kind of pissed with her or something."

"Actually, I didn't even want Karrin to come."

"Why not?"

"Because she's doing something low down."

"Low down like what?"

Lauren sighed. "She's flirting with Greg behind Toni's back."

Serita's jaw dropped and she reared back. "What? And Toni and she seem like such good friends."

"Toni thinks they are. Toni works with her at the school just as I do and adores the girl. But Greg has been telling Damien that she's been saying things to him behind Toni's back—things one friend should not say to another's fiancé. Worse, she let him see her naked in the shower and tried to tease him."

"Oh, my goodness! I can see why you're ticked off at her. Why did you invite her?"

"I didn't. Toni told her about the trip after we invited her and Greg. And then Karrin asked me about it. It didn't seem right not to ask her. She has been a good friend to me. But what she's doing behind Toni's back is as dirty as hell!"

"It sure is."

"If she'll do it to her, she'll do it to me, too!" Lauren tugged her shades up by the middle. "You know what I mean?"

"Of course."

"I just pray she doesn't act the fool on this trip."

"Me, too. Toni is so nice."

"Isn't she though? But so are you."

Serita blushed. "So are you sweetie."

"And if Hunter is interested in you and you in him, why not pursue it?"

"Last night we almost kissed, but Karrin said something about—"

"Karrin! Girl, don't let her steal your joy. Don't let anyone steal your happiness. Don't be afraid of Hunter. I see the way he looks at you, and speaks to you, and acts with you, it's precious. Don't throw it away. And I see how you act around him. Give it a chance. He may be the blessing God has sent specifically to you."

Inside the Buena Vista, Toni and Karrin also stood from the table, deciding to spend some time at a spa. As they walked away, the men remained at the table. Hunter noticed Greg watching them closely, before he turned back to face Damien and him. A wide grin spread across his thin face.

"She's doing it again," he uttered, throwing Damien a knowing look.

"Oh, man, shut up," Damien remarked.

Hunter looked bewildered for a moment and then looked like something dawned on him. "You're still talking about getting with Karrin? Please tell me, no."

Greg leaned toward Hunter, bursting with excitement. "Hey, what can I say? She wants me. She told me so this morning. She wants me badly."

Hunter waved his hand at him. "Man, you can't fall for that."

"We had breakfast on the beach and she was all over me."

Hunter looked at Damien's plump face. "Has he lost his mind?"

Damien sighed. "I keep telling him to stop it. He's thinking about playing with fire if he's thinking about messing around with his fianceé's friend."

"What are you getting married for, man?" Hunter asked.

Greg smirked at him. "Are you jealous?"

"Jealous of what?"

"Jealous of me getting ready to hit it. I know how you used to love to tap that."

"Hey, if you want her, you can have her. I just think you're really messing up with a nice lady like Toni." With that, Hunter stepped away from the table, shaking his head. "I'm going to look around outside."

Damien stood. "Hey, wait up, man. I'm hanging with you, too."

* * *

Later, after everyone returned to the villa, they dressed up in their finest and headed to the Crystal Palace Casino. As the travelers scattered about seeking their game of choice, Serita found herself accompanied by Hunter. They played the slots, poker and other games. All the while, they laughed, talked and whooped and hollered if they won. By the time he expressed wanting to go somewhere quiet to talk, Serita nor he had gained any winnings. They had just about broken even.

Serita cared less as they strolled outside in front of the enchanting resort that housed the casino. The mild island breeze floated through the air. They basked in it walking aimlessly and talking about their dreams, careers, and his family. Serita laughed until her stomach hurt when he told her about growing up in the Larimore household. And she appreciated him so much. Despite how overwhelmed with grief she felt about Chris the other night, somehow being around Hunter had made her forget her pain. Somehow, he made her feel more alive than ever. Serita ached to kiss his lips and wrap her arms around his body so badly that it would have tortured her not to return his affection on this night.

"I really like being with you," he confessed, gazing at her face. "You're a beautiful woman, Serita. Beautiful to look at, but beautiful inside as well. Just pure beautiful."

"I really like being with you, too, Hunter. You're beautiful, too."

Then suddenly he stepped close to her and bent his face toward hers. Swift breaths blew on her cheeks and she knew he felt the same from her since her heart beat so wildly. Then, as if a piece of heaven touched her, his butter-smooth lips met with hers.

As they glided across her mouth ever so sensuously, Hunter enfolded her up within his muscular arms. Serita couldn't resist wrapping her arms around his broad shoulders and sliding her hands along his arms to indulge herself in the luscious feeling of how solid and strong he felt. Serita's heart pounded far more savagely. And when his tongue pierced the opening of her lips, the inmost part of her throbbed with need to feel him down inside of her.

Hunter's embrace tightened. Drawing her deeper and deeper into him, his tongue swirled ravenously in Serita's mouth. She felt she would burst from the ecstasy she felt, especially when his huge firmness wedged into her clothed flesh. This feels too good, her body cried.

His scent, the feeling of his muscular body mashed against her soft one and the tantalizing way he thrilled her with his ravenous tongue made Serita climb the walls. As his erotic hunger grew for her, Serita felt him tasting her as if he couldn't get enough. Neither could she get enough of him. As their tongues danced hungrily, her hands grew bolder, as did his. They wandered all over his back and arms while his slid up and down her waist, stopping short at the top of her buttocks. It all made Serita feel a pressure in the base of her stomach that ached for relief.

"Oh, baby," he moaned between his mouth and hers.

Oh, baby is right, her sweltering body cried inside again and again and again.

Hours later, Serita and Hunter returned to the villa and went to their respective rooms. As she shed her clothes and slipped into a big T-shirt a huge grin lit up her face. The last thing she expected from this trip was to meet a wonderful man. She had anticipated spending time with Lauren and sightseeing for amusement. Now, she had been kissed so passionately, she didn't know whether she was coming or going. Hunter had excited her so much that it took all of her strength not to go to his room and make love to him. If he made love like he kissed, then they would never get out of bed. They had actually stood in one spot kissing for hours. It was the best thing that happened to her in a long time.

Still glowing from her encounter with Hunter, Serita made her way to the bedroom's bathroom when suddenly she saw her door open. Hunter didn't seem like the type just to barge in her room, but it was okay if he had. Yet it wasn't him. Karrin strolled in. She shut the door and shuffled across the room toward Serita.

"You have an extra soap?" she asked with a strange smile.

"I'll check." Serita strode into the bathroom and returned to Karrin with a bar of soap.

"Thanks," Karrin said, accepting the bar.

Serita smiled. "Anytime."

Karrin just stood there after that, still granting Serita that peculiar grin. That is, until she plopped down on the side of the bed. "So you were hanging with Hunter tonight, huh? I saw you two leave the casino together."

Serita felt uncomfortable about her interest, but answered anyway. "Yes, it was fun tonight."

"How fun?"

Serita reared back at her nosiness. "Just fun."

"Did he try to get you in bed?"

"No," Serita answered hesitantly.

Karrin raised her high arched brows. "I'm surprised."

"And why is that?"

"Because when Hunter is really, really attracted to a woman, he just can't keep his hands off her."

"We haven't known each other that long."

"That doesn't matter. When I just met him, he wanted me the first night."

"So I guess it didn't work out too well since you're not together anymore."

Karrin's nostrils flared and the smug expression left her face. "He still wants me. He knocked at my door a few minutes ago, but I turned him down."

"Oh, really."

"Of course."

"Well, that's your business."

"Yes, it is," she shot and flitted out the door, leaving it open.

Serita shook her head and closed the door.

Down the hall, Karrin stormed into her room. After closing the door, she paced across the floor and even kicked the wall several times. She could not figure out how in the world Hunter could prefer Serita's company to hers. She was more beautiful, sexier, more fun and an expert as far as pleasing a man. What he needed was a little reminder of just what he was missing.

Hours later, when Hunter lay in his bedroom at the villa, he couldn't stop thinking about Serita. Kissing her and touching her body had driven him crazy. He would have stood there kissing her and holding that gorgeous creature until morning if people leaving the casino hadn't passed by them. God knows, she had made him feel alive in a way that he had never felt before. He couldn't even bear for the time with her to end.

He would have loved to have spent the night in her room and discovered if they were compatible in other ways. He had been tempted to ask her to make love to him. Yet he knew he had to restrain his desire. The woman had lost her husband a year ago. She needed a little time.

Finally, Hunter had drifted off to sleep. Never a sound sleeper, as he turned to his left, he caught sight of his bedroom door opening and turned on his lamp. Karrin sashayed in, in a black, lacey sleep getup that barely covered her bottom.

"What's up?" he asked, sitting up.

Gazing at him softly, she pranced toward his bed. Hunter smelled her perfume before she even reached him. It smelled like the one she used to wear—Giorgio. He used to love it on her, but now he found the scent overpowering.

"I want to close the window in my room, but it seems stuck."

Hunter just looked at her for a moment. He hated to get out of his comfy bed. Yet he had been raised to be a gentleman.

Within a second, he strode inside Karrin's room, feeling the chill on his bare chest and even through his silk, pajama bottoms. When he grabbed the window, it came down so easily that he wondered if it had really been difficult to close. From experience, he knew all of Karrin's tricks. This time he tried to give her the benefit of the doubt.

"Thanks, Hunter."

"You're welcome." He started walking past her.

She shuffled in front of him, halting his steps. "Are you still angry with me? I didn't know it was forbidden to mention Serita's husband to her the other night."

Hunter sighed. "It's late, and I'm sleepy and tired. I really don't want to get into this."

"All I want to know is if you're mad at me? You act like it."

"No, it's all right," he said, trying to hide his annoyance.

"So will you spend time with me?"

"We're all spending time together."

"I don't mean in a group. I mean alone. Alone like you do with Serita. You need to give me another chance. I'm begging you."

"Karrin, I can't."

"Why?"

"Because we're not right for each other. We

just aren't. You deserve someone who will appreciate who you are. And I'm not that person. Someone out there is. I need someone who can appreciate who I am."

"I do appreciate you. You have no idea how much I do."

"You may think you do. But I need something else."

"No, you mean someone else," she said with a mixture of hurt and testiness. "Serita. You just want her because you never had her before. Because she's been playing with your head."

"I've had enough. Good night," he said firmly.

On that note, Hunter hurried down the hall. As he came closer to his room, he wondered again why in the world Lauren and Damien had invited her to come. The instant he saw Karrin's face, he saw trouble.

Down the hall, Serita lay in her bed in the dark with her eyes open. For a few minutes, she thought about that strange encounter with Karrin. Although the time spent with Hunter lingered in her mind foremost. It rendered her unable to sleep.

She couldn't stop reliving the way he kissed her in her mind. She couldn't get over how she felt at this moment just thinking about him. He was kind, funny, intelligent, ambitious and just too gorgeous and sexy.

Thinking of him, Serita drifted off into a pleasant dream. In it, Hunter entered her bedroom and approached her bed. But then suddenly, a dark energy came over her that unsettled her. Hunter vanished. In his place, a man with a ski mask stood over her. Moaning from the fright of the horrible dream, Serita wakened sweating, restless and frightened. The last time she had a nightmare, she'd dreamed that a monster hurt Chris.

But in reality, the monster had done more than hurt him. He had killed him. Rehashing it all made Serita feel afraid. She started to call out to Hunter. Then quickly she decided against that. She just couldn't cling to the first man since Chris who made her feel like he cared about her. And in spite of everything, Hunter did make her feel like he cared for her.

Chapter 9

The next morning when Serita saw the sky brushed with the orange-yellow-blue hues of sunrise, it surprised her that she woke so early. She had a long, eventful night and expected to sleep in late. From the soundlessness outside her bedroom door, she suspected that everyone else in the villa snoozed away.

Then again, she had always been an early riser. She loved to catch the world serene, so she could think and dream of beautiful things that lay beyond for her in the future. Often in Madera

Bay, she went for long walks, purely enjoying the country fresh air and getting some exercise. Yet here in Nassau-Paradise Island with that glorious beach right beyond the villa, she planned to soak up the sun and dip her body in the breathtakingly beautiful sea.

Soon after, Serita showered and picked out a lavender bathing suit that she'd designed to don on the beach. And minutes later, she left everyone slumbering and strode the short distance to the beach. A woman and a preteen boy played volleyball in the distance. Serita assumed they were mother and child, relishing the early morning like she did. She granted them a smile and spread a blanket on a spot not too far from the house, but near the ocean.

She relaxed on her back, feeling the maturing day's sunshine warming her skin. After closing her eyes for several seconds, she suddenly felt the thumps of feet and sensed a presence above her. The sun shined in her eyes, making her squint. Still she saw long, muscled legs, narrow hips and a buffed chest and arms of a heavenly vision. Her gaze traveled further upward and she saw Hunter staring at her.

"I was looking for you," he said, sitting beside her. "Lauren told me you were out getting some exercise. I like that you take care of yourself. It shows." He gave her body an admiring glance.

Serita smiled. "Oh, you like that, huh?"

He nodded and admired her bikini shamelessly. "Yes, indeed. And I must tell you with the swimsuit you have on today, I might have to be your bodyguard."

Serita chuckled. "Oh, really?"

"Oh, yes. It's just as beautiful as the one you wore on our first day on the island. That one you designed."

"I designed this one, too."

"Awesome. You're so talented. I really like it. And I like even better what's in it. You have a beautiful body."

Serita glowed. "Thank you. You're not bad yourself."

"And like I told you last night, you have a beautiful face." He raised his fascination to her eyes and lips.

Serita returned the hot scrutiny for a few moments until a ball rolled near her feet. Seeing it belonged to the boy at the other end of the beach, she stood and tossed it to him. Hunter stood with her.

"I think I've lain around long enough," she told Hunter. "It's about time I get into that water."

"Ah, you can't swim," he teased.

"You want to bet?" She ran down to the water. He ran after her.

Within the warm ocean, he chased her and they swam, and lastly engaged in a water fight. After the last time Serita splashed Hunter with water, he came after her. She ran and he captured her from behind. Instantly feeling his strong arms around her weakened her. Equally tantalizing, she felt every part of him and every part of him felt firm. She turned around and gazed in his face. The playful expression he had moments ago had faded. He just stared at her, dividing most of his captivation between her eyes and lips.

"What are you doing to me, Serita?"

"What are you doing to me?"

"You know I was thinking about you all last night."

"I did the same," she confessed breathlessly.

Just then, the mother and child enjoying the beach approached their direction. Hence, Serita and Hunter decided to head back over to the sand where they could be alone. Yet as they relaxed once again in the sand, she remembered something about the previous night. She tried not to. Still, it haunted her. She remembered what Karrin said.

"Are you and Karrin really over?"

"Of course. Why do you ask that? Did somebody say something?"

"Karrin did. Last night after we came back, she visited me in my room. Said she needed some soap, which I gave her. But she really wanted to talk about you."

Hunter smiled and grabbed Serita's hand. "Look, I don't even need to hear the rest. All I want you to know is that I'm not involved with that woman. Like I said, we used to date a few years ago after Lauren introduced us, but that's long been over. And there is no chance in the world anything will be rekindled. So if she implied that we were involved, she is very mistaken or just outright lying." He paused, gazing in Serita's eyes. "I'm interested in only one person."

With that Serita saw his gaze drop to her lips

and his face lean toward hers. Aching with need to taste the luscious gift of his lips again, Serita leaned closer to him.

Though, suddenly an approaching sight beyond his shoulder made her move back. Hunter curved his head to see who captured her attention. Toni and Lauren strode across the sand toward them.

"Hey, what's up?" Toni said, her coppery skin gleaming in the sun. She wore a large, straw hat flopped down over her short fro and a striped one-piece swimsuit.

Serita patted a spot beside her. "Come on, my sisters, and soak up the sun."

"Oh, no," Hunter joked. "I'm surrounded by women. Now, you'll are going to talk about hairstyles and clothes and recipes, and all that stuff."

"No, we're not," Toni said. "We're going to talk about you."

"Me? What about me?"

Toni reared back, gazing at him. "We want to know if you have changed your views on settling down and getting married."

Serita felt intrigued about Toni's remarks to Hunter and smiled awkwardly.

"Okay," Hunter said, standing. "Time for me to go for a swim."

All three women laughed. Hunter headed toward the ocean. As he began doing laps, Lauren's bright eyes shifted to Serita.

"Come on, girl, what's up? I saw you two."

"Maybe you'll be the one to drag Hunter Larimore to the altar," Toni teased.

Serita chuckled and again wondered why Toni made comments about Hunter and marriage. "No, we're just enjoying the beach."

"I see the way he looks at you," Toni added. "I'm very observant. You got him, girl."

"Umm huh," Lauren agreed. "That's why Karrin is walking around this morning with her mouth poked out."

"Oh, stop," Toni said, "leave her alone."

"Huh." Lauren twisted her mouth. "Leave her alone nothing. I didn't even want her to come."

"Why?" Toni asked.

"Because she does things that I don't agree with."

"Like what?"

To that, Lauren exchanged a quick glance with Serita. It made Serita recall what Lauren had told her. Karrin had been practically trying to seduce Greg.

"You know how she is," Lauren went on. "Always up in some man's face."

"Well, you know she loves men," Toni reasoned. "We can't fault her for that. She has a healthy sexual appetite I guess. Besides, we shouldn't be so hard on her. We've all had a man propose to us because he wants to share the rest of his life with us—and she hasn't. She's just looking for love like all of us women do."

To that, Lauren exchanged a quick glance with Serita again. Still, Serita felt intrigued about Toni's remarks about marriage.

"Well, she surely has a thing for Hunter," Serita said. "Did she want to marry him and he didn't want to marry her or something? Is that why you teased him about getting married?"

Toni grinned. "Yes, she did tell me she wanted to marry him. But also, everyone knows how Hunter is. He claims he will never ever get married. In fact, he claims that he has never been and will never fall in love. He says love isn't in his plans."

Lauren gave her a wary look. "Don't make him sound like a playboy."

"I'm not doing that," Toni countered.

"What it is," Lauren clarified, "is that he hasn't met the right woman yet. When he does, he'll change his mind." She threw Serita a smile. "He might be changing it already."

A few hours later, Hunter entered the villa unable to get Serita out of his head. He smiled thinking of how sexy she looked in that lavender bikini. Her rich, brown skin glistened beneath the island sun. The girl had curves that still had his temperature elevated. With that gorgeous face and that long, flowing hair down her back, set against the backdrop of the beach, she looked like some goddess.

He smiled, as he approached the kitchen, his grin faded. He overheard a conversation that made him stand out of sight and listen.

"So what do you like?" Karrin asked Greg.

"I like a lot of things."

"You know what I'm talking about?"

"Hey, I'm a man with an adventurous sex drive."

"And I'm a woman with one."

Greg laughed. "I can tell that."

"How?"

"Just by looking at you. You look like you got the magic."

"I do. I really know how to please a man. I bet Toni doesn't even do everything you like."

"You're right."

"I bet she doesn't do half of the things in bed you want her to do."

"She sure doesn't."

"Well, I like to do all sorts of freaky things. I'll do anything in bed to please my man—absolutely anything."

Having heard enough, Hunter headed to his room. He couldn't figure out why Greg wanted to ruin his relationship with Toni. Because that is exactly what Hunter predicted would happen. Greg was headed for disaster.

Damien, Greg and he had known each other since they all attended Howard University together. Of the three, Greg always acted recklessly. It led to him having many financial problems and being unemployed numerous times. In fact, he was an unemployed computer tech at this precise moment. It amazed him that Toni put up with him. Though, he guessed that she loved him.

Yet Hunter refused to worry about it. He planned to enjoy a game of basketball with Damien and later party on a cruise ship with the crew. He planned to spend every other second of his time with Serita.

Far away in Madera Bay, Mitchell sat in his office at the police station, poring over what he always preoccupied him whenever the workload became light on the island—the Evangeline Jones case. As he examined the old files, he thought of his father-in-law. Phillip Branson's statements along with those of two of his buddies pretty much sealed the case. When he'd questioned Phillip about it in private during the days when he was well and at home, the older man always clammed up. Yet Mitchell detected something in his expression that showed he hid something about the Jones case.

Recently, however, during Phillip's illness and Mitchell's last visit to his father-in-law at the hospital, Phillip clutched Mitchell's hand, making him stay in the room while the others left. When the two of them were alone, Phillip requested that Mitchell come visit him. He claimed that he had something to tell him about Evangeline Jones.

Since Mitchell knew that Julie and Victoria took a shopping trip to a new mall in Columbia, South Carolina, he believed today would be a good day to visit Phillip. Perhaps he could answer questions for him, especially one particular question—was Evangeline Jones dead, instead of a woman on the run as everyone believed? Through Mitchell's review of the case evidence that question had arisen in his mind. Yet only the men who were there that night the tragedy occurred would actually know the truth. Phillip Branson, his father-in-law was one of those men.

A short while later, Mitchell walked in Madera Bay General Hospital. After reaching the eighth floor, he stopped at the nurse's desk for them to page Phillip Branson's doctor. Mitchell wanted to ask his doctor if it was okay to speak to his father-in-law about a stressful subject. Although Phillip Branson wanted to discuss it, Mitchell didn't want to do anything to put the older man's health in jeopardy.

As he stood in hallway waiting, Mitchell saw his brother-in-law, Rod, walking down the hall toward him.

"Hey, brother-in-law," Rod addressed Mitchell. "What are you doing here?"

"Waiting to talk to your father's doctor and then see him if I can."

Rod dabbed at the side of his bald head. "Since when did you get so interested in my father's condition? Julie send you or something?"

"No, Julie didn't send me."

"Then what are you doing here? I mean it's all right for you to see my father, but what do you need to talk to his doctor for? His condition is a family matter."

"I thought I was family."

"You're not his son or daughter. You're just a guy who got lucky and married into a rich family."

Mitchell chuckled. "Thanks for making me feel so welcome as always."

"You should know by now that I tell it like I see it. And from what I see, you made out pretty damn well by marrying my sister."

"I don't want Julie's money. I earn my own."

"Oh, that's right. You do play cop on an island that hardly has any crime."

"Oh, I'm never bored. Sometimes one crime can take years and years to solve."

Rod's deep-set eyes knotted up like claws. "Now what is that supposed to mean?"

"It means I have business to take care of."

Just then, a beautiful, Latino nurse approached Mitchell. "Detective Lane, Mr. Branson's doctor is with another patient and won't be available for another two hours."

Rod stepped among them. "That's all right. This man shouldn't be speaking to my daddy's doctors anyway."

"As an officer of the law, I do have a right to question your father." He then switched his attention to the nurse. "Thank you for that information. I'll come back another time."

Rod frowned. "Like hell you will. You sound like you're questioning my daddy about a police matter. He hasn't done anything. The poor man is deathly ill and you're trying to harass him and sending him to his rest that much faster. What is this about?"

"If it concerned you, I would tell you. Have a good day, brother-in-law."

After leaving the hospital, Mitchell sat in his squad car for several seconds thinking about Rod's protectiveness about his father. He wondered if he feared him taking the family fortune. Well, Rod need not worry. Money was the last thing he wanted from the Branson family. In fact, he doubted that he even wanted Julie anymore.

Less than an hour later, Mitchell drove down a back road en route to visit another elderly gentleman who may have known what actually happened to Evangeline Jones. Gilbert Edwards had been there during the night of the Evangeline Jones incident, along with his friend, Cedric Vonrich. However, Mr. Vonrich had been deceased for several years.

After driving up into the unkempt yard, Mitchell knocked on the door of a home that was equally scruffy. Once he knocked, Gilbert opened the door looking angry.

"What do you want?" he asked, his blue eyes glancing out at the squad car and then at Mitchell.

"I'm Detective Mitchell Lane and I would like to ask you some questions."

"Questions about what?"

"Can I come in and discuss it further?"

"No, I was in the middle of something."

Mitchell heard the television playing in the house. "Yes, I'm sure you're a very busy man. In fact, you worked for Phillip Branson at his soda factory, right?"

"So what if I did."

"So you were there during the Evangeline Jones situation."

Hearing those words caused Gilbert's chest to heave and his nostrils to flare. "I don't have nothing to say about that mess."

"Why? Why can't you just tell me what happened like you told the police years ago right after it happened?"

"Because I told the story once and it's no need to dredge up that dirt again."

"You seem mighty bothered, Mr. Edwards."

"Because I told you I was in the middle of something. Now go on."

Gilbert slammed the door in Mitchell's face. Mitchell knocked on the door to question him again. Gilbert refused to answer. Mitchell hopped back in his car. As he drove down the road headed back to the station, he knew his instincts were right. There was more to the Evangeline Jones story—much more than had been originally told. There was the interesting evidence that intrigued him. There were the strange reactions and behavior of those involved. Most importantly, there was Serita. She swore that her mother hadn't abandoned her or did what everyone accused her of.

His buddies at the police station called him foolish for immersing himself in the case. But the more he reviewed the evidence, encountered those involved and remembered Serita's face as she expressed her thoughts about her mother, he knew an injustice had been done that he had to see corrected.

Mitchell also knew something else. He had to solve this case. He had to solve it for Serita. With the hurt he had inflicted on her, he felt compelled to give her this one gift of really knowing what happened to her mother. It was the least he could do.

During the evening, Serita, Hunter, Lauren, Damien, Toni, Greg and Karrin boarded the

Vargas Party Ship. Sailing out to sea beneath a starry sky, Serita savored an array of cuisine ranging from American, Greek, Polynesian to Chinese and Mexican. When she tasted one of Bahamas's native dishes, conch, she fell in love with the tasty shellfish.

The music thrilled her as well. She danced with Damien, Greg and Hunter to booty shaking Caribbean beats. As well, the disc jockey played lots of American music, especially R&B classics. When the Ojay's slow groove "Stairway to Heaven" came on Hunter grabbed her hard and led her to the dance floor.

"I refuse to share you with Damien and Greg on this one," he teased. "This is my song."

Serita looked at him amazed. "This is my song, too."

Within seconds, Hunter found them a spot among the crowded slow-moving bodies. He wrapped his arms around her and Serita slid her hands on his shoulders. Feeling them, she couldn't get over how hard he felt. And as he moved close to her sealing her against him, she couldn't get over how hard he felt in a certain spot. The shock made her look up into his eyes, he gazed down in hers, as if silently telling her to "see what you did to me."

Yet if only he knew what he did to her as well. With every torrid sway of their bodies, her body ached with aroused sensations. How could she have just met this man and allowed him to have such an affect on her? It blew her mind.

The sultry flutters down within her grew intense as the song and his moves progressed. Hunter held her so tightly and moved so sexily, Serita couldn't resist holding him tighter as well. Clinging to him, her nose brushed his chest and she inhaled the coconut scent that he must have rubbed on his hair and elsewhere on his body. Coconut had never smelled so heavenly.

They danced to a few more slow jams and Serita would have continued for the next. However, the disc jockey decided to play an up-tempo tune again. Addicted to Hunter, Serita had to dance with him on those tunes, too. She had a wonderful time. The only dim point came when she glanced at Karrin who stood at a distance watching them. As usual, her eyes burned into Serita's flesh.

Ignoring her, Serita was intent to enjoy

herself. When a band began playing, the evening really heated up. They performed lots of R&B, pop and jazz classics. Afterward they even invited audience members on stage to sing. It didn't take much coaxing for Hunter to get up on stage. He grabbed the microphone and asked them to play "The Closer I Get to You" and Serita became spellbound. As Hunter sang the lyrics in a rich, baritone voice, he stared at her. Lauren, Damien, Greg and Toni all cheered him on from the audience. Yet Serita felt too speech-less from the beautiful words sung to her and the beautiful voice behind it. Chills shivered through her spine. At his finale, all the dancers gave him a standing ovation.

"I didn't know you could sing like that," Serita gushed after he returned to her.

"Me, either," he joked. "You were my inspi-ration."

Lauren, Greg, Toni and Damien joined them in praising his performance while Karrin stood aside still looking angry. Serita watched Hunter blushing like a young boy from all the compli-ments before he whisked her away to a secluded section of the boat.

As they stood near a rail, he admitted, "I couldn't have sung like that if I didn't have a reason."

"And what's your reason?" Serita asked.

"You. The closer I get to you, the more I feel things."

"What kind of things?"

"Things—things like I've never felt before. And you do, too, don't you?"

Serita looked down and then back up at him. "Yes, I do. And I feel guilty."

"Why?"

"Because my husband died a year ago and here I am feeling things and becoming involved with someone else."

"Serita, don't do this to yourself." He held the sides of her arms. "I'm sure if you loved this man the way you do and he was a good man."

"He was a good man. A very good man."

"Then a good man wouldn't want his mate to grieve forever. He would want the best for her. He would want her to enjoy all the beauty of life. A year is not a short amount of time. Besides, I feel that it was our destiny to meet."

Serita thought about what he said, and then

remembered what Toni said at the beach. "Have you ever been in love, Hunter?"

"No."

"Do you hate the idea of marriage?"

"No, I don't hate it. My parents are happily married. It's just that everyone else I know has a terrible time with it."

"So you don't plan to ever get married?"

He hesitated. "I guess not."

"I see." She gazed off in the direction of the water, but saw none of it. All she saw was in her mind's eye. She was falling for a man who had no intentions of anything serious, only a fling.

"I'm not a player," he said as if reading her mind. "I mean, some people might see me that way, but I'm not. I treat women very well. If I am seeing one, I don't lead her on or hurt her. And I don't plan to do that to you. But believe me when I tell you that I've never had feelings like I do for you, for any other woman. You're making me question all that I believed."

Serita smiled and she thought about what Lauren said. Perhaps he hadn't met the right woman yet. "I really like you, Hunter. Just don't hurt me."

"Oh, baby," he said, bringing his lips to hers. "I'd never hurt you.

With that, Hunter held her and kissed her. Serita embraced him in return. His lips caressed hers in a butterfly motion until his tongue slipped in her mouth. She welcomed him into her warm honey and he tasted her as if she addicted him. Before long, Hunter's tongue did a sensuous motion that simulated the erotic motions of lovemaking. With each move, he moaned and she felt his chest heave.

Serita's lower body throbbed with need. Inhaling his intoxicating coconut scent, she hoped this moment would last forever. And as they stood their kissing, time ceased to exist.

After Serita returned to the villa that evening, she entered her bedroom exhausted and extremely excited. She couldn't get over how much Hunter turned her on. Dancing with him had been fun enough. His singing to her made the night all the more incredible. Yet the last part of their evening, when he kissed her so passionately again, had been the best part of the night. She was so turned on—turned on to a man who didn't even want marriage. What was she getting into?

* * *

Not far away, Hunter raided the villa's refrigerator for the last of the orange juice, his favorite drink, and then made his way to his bedroom. As he walked, he couldn't stop thinking of Serita. Neither would he stop desiring her.

Tonight, she had made him so hot on the dance floor that he almost burst from the excitement. He loved the way she moved her body and couldn't stop wondering about her moving like that if they made love. And then when he sang to her, he felt the words in every part of his soul, especially when he looked in her beautiful eyes. And he did mean every word. The closer he got to her, the more he knew they just couldn't be friends. And with the way he felt when he kissed her, he wondered if she was even making him forget his vows of avoiding love and marriage. Because in his heart, something strange was happening.

Reaching his dark bedroom, he knew he would have to take a cold, cold shower. Yet when he flipped on the light switch, he realized that would have to wait. Karrin lay in his bed beneath the covers. Seductively she smiled at him and

lifted the spread from her body. She was naked.
Her nightgown and kimono were on the floor.

"Get in, lover," she whispered.

Chapter 10

"Why are you acting this way, Karrin?" Hunter asked, frowning at the naked woman in his bed.

"Why do you think? Because I want you just as much as you want me. Admit it. You know you're too hot right now."

"I want you to put on your clothes and to leave right now."

Her hazel eyes raked over his body. "Why? Because you're scared you'll jump my bones at any second?"

"I would like you to get out."

Her face fell. "You don't mean that."

"Oh, yes, I do."

"You can't tell me you're not excited right now. You know I look good and you want me."

"You're a beautiful woman, I won't deny that. But I'm no longer interested."

"Because of what I did?"

"Because we're in the past."

She stood and started over to him.

"Put your clothes on," he told her again.

"Why? You are tempted, aren't you?"

When she reached him and tried to brush against him, he hurried over to her slinky robe. He picked it up and handed it to her.

Clearly disappointed, she slipped on her the kimono. Yet she would not leave.

"Hunter, I still have feelings for you," she confessed, standing in front of him. "I still think about you. That's why I wanted to come on this trip so badly. It would give me a chance to see you again and to make things right."

"I don't want to get into this."

"Please, just listen. We had something good once."

"Yes, we did."

"I missed you."

"Karrin, please."

"And I love you."

Hunter just looked at her.

"And I know you can't say it back. You never did. But it's okay. Even if you can't say, I know that you love me, too."

"Is that what you really believe?"

"Yes. And I don't even care if you can't or won't say it. I love you any way. I've never met a man like you. You're gorgeous. You're sexy. You have it all together and you're funny and I love your personality. And I love the way you make love to me. No man before or after ever made love to me like you did. I never felt that way with anyone else. And I want to feel that way again."

She moved close to Hunter, rubbing his arms. "Hunter, I know what I did for you, too. I drove you wild and you know it. No one turned you on like I did."

Hunter stared at her. She looked beautiful. Added to it, he had to admit that, sexually, their compatibility blew his mind. Still, she had hurt him. And now he was grateful she had. His interest lay elsewhere. The spell Serita worked on him tonight made him unable to react to a beautiful woman offering herself to him in her bare flesh.

"I'm interested in someone else," he admitted.

Karrin's nostrils flared. "Oh, please."

"I'm just being honest."

"No, you're just trying to hurt me because I hurt you in the past."

"Woman, I'm not even thinking about the past. I'm thinking about the future."

"A future with Ms. Boring."

"I have no idea who you're referring to."

"That boring Serita. What is it? Because you can't even compare her with me."

"You are so insecure. Why do you say things like that?"

"Are you into being with people because you feel sorry for them?"

"What are you talking about?"

"I heard about her getting shot and about her husband being killed."

"So what?"

"So you're feeling sorry for her."

"Anybody will feel empathy for such a tragedy, but I spent time with her and I'm spending more time with her because I love her company. Now would you leave please?"

Karrin rolled her eyes at him and stormed out the door, leaving it open.

Moments later, Karrin paced inside her room fuming. Hunter had insulted her for the last time. As she moved from one part of the floor to another, now her thoughts turned to revenge. She wanted Hunter to pay for mistreating her. Equally, she wanted Serita to hurt for flaunting herself and luring him away. She would think of something for her. Yet as for Hunter, she knew a way to get back at him—with his friend. One thing a man couldn't stand was to see his buddy screwing a woman that he had been with.

With that in mind, she headed down to the living room. She knew Greg hung out down there with the others. And when she walked into the room, he was the first one who looked up from the cable movie that had them all engrossed.

"Come join us," he said.

Toni glimpsed. "Yes, come on, girl." She patted a spot next to her on the sofa. "This is so good. It's a thriller that you just can't stop watching."

"I would," Karrin said, "but I...I have a big bug in my room, and I wanted to know if one of the guys could get it out." She looked at Greg. "Can you?"

"Sure he can," Toni answered. "Go help her get that critter out, baby. Because before you know it, if you don't get it, all of us will have bugs in our rooms."

After walking out of the living room with Karrin, Greg asked, "What kind of bug did it look like?"

Karrin grinned at him instead of answering.

Greg got the message and smiled. "Want to walk on the beach?" he whispered. "Toni is going to be watching that movie for a long time."

Karrin rolled her tongue around her lips. "Sounds perfect to me."

The next day for lunch, Serita and everyone dined at The Bahamian Kitchen. The island's native dishes were served there and the food made her mouth water. After everyone had happily stuffed themselves, they sat around the table talking about the fun on the yacht the previous night.

"Serita stepped all over my toes," Hunter said making everyone laugh.

"When?" she asked smiling at him.

"When we danced of course."

"No, you were the one stepping on my toes with those big feet."

Lauren, Damien, Greg and Toni chuckled. Karrin threw her eyes heavenward.

Hunter reared back in his chair, staring across at Serita with twinkling eyes. "Ah, you're just mad because I'm the better dancer."

"You're delusional, Mr. Larimore. I am the better dancer."

"Yeah, she is the better dancer," Lauren added.

"Didn't you see my graceful moves?" Serita toyed with him.

"Yes, and I wondered how did you move all that."

"All what?"

"All that junk in your trunk."

Everyone cracked up accept Karrin. Again, her hazel eyes rolled toward the heavens.

"You shouldn't be looking there," Serita said laughing.

"Hey, I'm a man. I look."

"And why do you men look at women's butts all the time anyway?" Lauren asked. "What are they looking for?"

"The roundness," Damien said, forming a circle with his hands and making everyone laugh.

Greg nodded in agreement. "And the tightness, too. I don't like no jiggle butt."

Everyone laughed again, except for Karrin.

"What's the matter with you, girl?" Toni addressed her. "Why aren't you having any fun?"

"I'm having fun," she said, "but I was wondering something."

"What?" Toni asked.

Karrin looked across the table at Serita. "How could you sit here laughing?"

Serita scowled. "Why are you asking me that?"

"Because I heard that your husband tried to kill you before he killed himself."

Serita gasped at the dig at her heart.

Lauren glared at Karrin. "What's wrong with you? Why would you want to bring Serita and everyone else down by saying something like that?"

"Because she's thoughtless!" Hunter snapped.

Karrin shot him a dirty look, and then

switched her attention back to Serita. "If my husband tried to kill me, I—"

"My husband didn't try to kill me," Serita said.

"And I didn't tell you that," Lauren said to Karrin. "I told you that my friend was shot and her husband killed and the police thought he did it, but she knows he didn't."

"But if the police think so," Karrin went on, "obviously they have evidence that supports that accusation."

Chapter 11

"Why are you saying this?" Lauren raged.

"Because I have a right to say what I damn well please!"

"You're awful," Hunter stated.

Karrin's nostrils flared. "You can be pretty awful yourself, Mr. Hunter Larimore, player of the year."

"You're a mess, Karrin," Lauren continued. "An absolute mess."

"I'm no more of a mess than anyone here. Don't tell me that none of you haven't wondered if the dude shot her then shot himself."

Serita leaned across the table toward Karrin, baffled at how someone could behave so horribly. "Don't you dare refer to my husband as a dude and don't you dare say he did anything. You don't know any damn thing about him!"

"I know enough," Karrin said with a smirk. "You sure got over him fast."

"You don't know anything about what's in my heart."

Lauren gazed at Serita softly. "Serita, I'm sorry I told her anything."

"It's all right," Serita said to Lauren. She stood. "I have to go to the ladies' room. I'll be back."

Once inside the ladies' room, Serita gazed in the mirror and saw the tears welling up in her eyes. After dabbing them away and blotting her face with a cold tissue, she felt a bit more refreshed. As soon as she stepped out the door, she saw Hunter standing there.

"I thought you might need some company," he said.

"Thank you."

"Let's go for a walk."

"All right."

Hunter slipped his arm around her waist and Serita felt herself relax.

"I'm so sorry she did that to you."

"She is just too terrible."

"She's jealous."

"And it shows. She seems more jealous than ever. What brought that on? I know that she saw us dancing on the boat and she didn't seem to like it."

"It's something else," Hunter said.

Serita looked aside at him. "Like what?"

"She tried to seduce me last night. When I returned to my room, I found her naked in my bed."

"Oh, my God."

"I told her that I'm interested in you and that I had no intention of being with her. I think that pushed her over the edge and you see the result of that today. Karrin can be very spiteful."

"I see that."

"That's one of her personality traits that turned me off. But your personality as well as everything else about you turns me on." He stared at her and caressed her cheek as they strolled. "Don't you ever worry about her again. 'Cause I'll be there."

"You will?"

"Oh, yes. I plan to be around you as much as I can. Now, let's not waste our time together talking about her. Let's talking about something beautiful."

"Sounds good to me."

Serita took a deep breath of contentment and continued to stroll down the island street with Hunter. He began talking about things that immediately uplifted her, quickly making her forget the ugliness at the table. It all made her realize, Hunter Larimore had become her angel.

In Madera Bay, Mitch strode through the Branson mansion to the pool area in the back. He had just left work and before he did, Julie phoned him telling him to pick her up at her folks' place. Her BMW had a problem and had been towed to the shop.

Once he reached the backyard, he anticipated seeing Julie doing laps across the pool. She loved swimming. Instead, she sat huddled with Rod, at a patio table. A slew of papers covered it.

Mitchell walked up to the table. "What's all this?"

"Hi, honey," Julie said, glancing up at him.

"It's our business matters," Rod answered. "Nothing for you to worry about. Why don't you take a seat over there?" He pointed at a faraway table.

"I'll be another minute," Julie said.

Mitchell took the seat his brother-in-law offered him. Sitting there, he also studied him. At only thirty-five, Rod's head had become bald and his face appeared wrinkled. Rod was not aging well. Mitchell assumed that is what happened to a person when they devoted their time trying to make others miserable.

Mitchell didn't need to sit at the table with Julie and Rod to know what they toiled away on. Julie had shared with him that since their father's hospitalization, Rod concentrated on keeping their companies thriving. The best way he felt to do this was by cutting salaries, increasing employee hours and cutting benefits. Rod strived to give his employees as little as he could get away with. He felt his father behaved too generously to the people who worked for him. Oddly enough, Julie agreed.

Hours later, at their home, Julie talked nonstop about the enterprises and the way Rod and she planned to cut costs and increase their profits. It bored Mitchell, though he kept his feelings to himself. And even when they were alone in their bedroom with his naked flesh pressed against hers, she still failed to interest him. She loved him passionately, giving him her all as always. Still, as their bodies rocked together, he couldn't stop his mind from wandering elsewhere. He couldn't stop it from wandering to another time with another woman.

On Nassau-Paradise Island, beneath a vibrant sun and gentle breeze, Serita and Hunter enjoyed a sports outing. He had invited her to join him as soon as they met up at the breakfast table that morning. He still wanted to cheer her up since Karrin behaved so nastily to her.

Their first adventure took them to the championship golf courses, where Serita took lessons from Hunter. Next, they had a workout at the tennis courts, in which Serita beat Hunter. Lastly, they wound up the day riding together on a scooter until well into the night.

They topped off their exciting day with a long, lingering kiss.

Exhilarated from all the fun with Hunter during the day, Serita returned to her room exhausted. She plopped down on the bed in an instant. When she heard a knock on the door, she had no energy to sit up. She simply commanded the visitor, "Come in."

Hunter looked too energetic, she thought as he nearly bopped into her room.

He laughed at her pooped state. "Can't take it, huh?"

"I took it."

"Girl, you're knocked out."

"No, I'm not."

"Why don't you just admit that I wore you out today and I still have energy."

Serita's lips curled gently. "All right. You win. You're the better sportsmen, even though I beat you at tennis."

"Oh, I know you were going to bring that up."

Suddenly he became quiet. She saw his eyes traveling over her body.

"You're really knocked out, aren't you?"

"Oh, yes. I'm pooped."

He grinned. "Why don't you let me do something about that?"

"Something like what? What can you do for a tired body?"

"Give it a good massage."

"Oh," Serita thought aloud, loving the idea, but at the same time afraid of it. Every time he touched her today, her hand, her waist, her arm, anywhere, she felt herself slipping over the cliff of control. And when he kissed her, her body had mad cravings for more and more. What would his massage do to her?

Before she could answer herself, Hunter eased toward the bed with a serious expression. She rolled on her stomach to give him good access to her tired back. The instant he touched it, she knew he had the magic touch.

"Umm, that's good."

"I knew you would like that."

His fingers kneaded her back more, up by her shoulders, armpits, at the mid back and below. When he reached the bottom of her back where she felt tense, her sweat suit pants prevented his access.

"You can pull it down some," she told him.

Granted permission, Hunter did as she

asked. His finger pressed into the top of her hips so expertly that she wanted him to massage even lower.

Chapter 12

Knowing she wasn't ready for the ultimate intimacy, Serita knew she had to turn around and end this moment before things got out of hand. Though, when she swung around, Hunter stared down in her face with lust-drugged eyes. She gazed at his lips, aching to taste them. He answered her unasked plea and brought his face close to hers.

But just then, the door opened, making him move back and Serita sit up.

Damien's chubby face blushed with embarrassment as he held on to the doorknob. "I should have knocked. My bad. Sorry."

"It's okay," Serita said.

"I was looking for you, Hunter. You have a call from your brother."

"Which one?"

"My man Tyler."

"You mean the pest," he said with a grin, and then as if realizing something, his amusement faded. "Everything is all right, isn't it?"

"Yes, he said everyone's cool. I asked. He said he just needs to talk to you about something concerning the restaurant. I think he just misses your butt and wanted to talk to you and see how the trip is going."

Serita's eyes sparkled. "That's so nice."

"No, it isn't," Hunter said in a lighthearted tone. "He probably wants to bug me about something."

Reluctantly he headed to the door and gazed back at her. When he closed the door behind him, Serita felt dreamy. She could understand his family missing him. She missed him, too, and he had just left her a second ago.

Moments later, she relaxed in the dark, obsessed with thoughts of Hunter—the prevailing one being making love to him. Yet how could she even consider a deeper involvement with him. She believed in love and marriage. He believed in being with someone for the moment and having a good time.

After speaking to Tyler about restaurant matters, Hunter headed back to Serita's room. As he strode down the hall, he heard laughter outside one of the windows. Planning to tease the amused ones and tell them to cut that out, he stuck his head out the window. He saw Karrin and Greg out in front of the house. When Karrin noticed him at the window, she immediately leaned toward Greg and plowed one on his lips. Hunter shook his head and continued down the hall to Serita's room. Poor Toni was all he thought.

"So I hope you missed me," Hunter teased Serita once they reunited in her room.

"A lot," she said, smiling. He eased toward her, hoping they could pick up where they left off. Yet she looked so beautiful, he just couldn't resist leaning close to her and kissing her. Sweeping his arms around her, he felt her arms coming around him, too. Loving it, he kissed her more passionately and felt sensations that overwhelmed him. Wanting to touch and feel all of her, he caressed her back, arms, neck and then eased his hands toward her cleavage. As his hand wandered lower, Serita tensed up and moved back.

"I'm not ready for more."

Hunter exhaled. "I am, but I'm patient. You're worth waiting for."

"Thank you."

"Now, how about that massage?"

She giggled.

"What?"

"I just think a massage would work things up right now. How about watching a good movie?"

"What kind do you like?"

"Thrillers."

Hunter grinned. "Those are my favorite, too. Let's go. I'll get the popcorn."

Outside in front of the villa, Karrin tried to enjoy herself with Greg. Despite it, each time she kissed him, she felt about excited as she would if she kissed a wall. The only thing about it was that Hunter witnessed her affection toward Greg. She hoped he fumed over it and thought about her as he spent the evening with Serita. She knew that's where he was headed. As she saw Toni and Lauren getting out of a taxicab after a shopping spree, she knew her fun with Greg would be over for the evening. Even so, she had more fun planned. If she seduced Greg, and did it extremely well, surely he would tell Hunter. Men loved to brag about their exploits. The thought of that happening made her day.

The next day Hunter, Damien and Greg embarked on a boys' day out. Hunter yearned to go scuba diving and suggested his buddies accompany him. It turned out to be an electrifying experience. Beneath the ocean, they explored, discovering colorful tropical fish, coral gardens, ocean caves, shallow reefs and even old sunken ships. They spent hours enjoying their dive.

Once they finished, they were ravenous. They scanned the restaurants located near the marina. That's when Hunter spotted Karrin. She walked alone and sashayed over to them.

"What are you guys doing over this way?" she asked.

Greg beamed. "We went scuba diving."

"Wow," she remarked. "That sounds like fun."

"It was," Damien told her.

"Next time you guys go, I want to come."

"Why don't you go with the ladies?" Hunter asked.

Karrin glared at him. "I'll go with who I want to go with." She clutched Greg's skinny arm. "Maybe I'll go with you."

Greg's grin widened. "I'd love to take you, baby doll."

Hunter and Damien exchanged irritated looks in response to Greg and Karrin's exchange.

"And maybe we can do something else fun afterward, like go dancing at one of the clubs. I saw your moves on the boat the other night. You can move that sexy body."

Greg's grin widened even more. Damien and Hunter eyed each other again.

"Whatever you want, baby doll," Greg agreed.

"No, baby," she said, brushing his cheek with her palm. "It's whatever you want. You can have it and I mean that sincerely. See you'll now."

With that, she walked away, switching her

hips extra hard and tossing her lengthy dark blond locks.

Greg could barely breathe because of his excitement. "That girl has been putting the lip-lock on me like nobody's business. Now, did you'll hear what she said to me?"

"Yes, I heard it," Damien replied. "She's playing with you."

"No, she's not."

"She is," Hunter countered. "She was in my room the other night telling me she loved me."

Greg frowned. "So."

"So nothing," Hunter said with aggravation in his voice. "She's playing you to make me jealous."

Greg shook his head. "No, she's not."

"She is, man," Damien agreed with Hunter.

"She wants me."

"She wants to make a fool out of any man she can," Hunter informed him. "You need to wake up and treasure what you have."

"I treasure Toni. She's a good woman. But, hey, look at Karrin. I know her pretty butt is something else between the sheets." He gazed at Hunter for confirmation.

Hunter shook his head. "You're foolish."

"And you're crazy for not tapping that the other night. When she lets me, I'm going to put it to her."

Damien and Hunter eyed her and shook their heads.

That evening Hunter returned to the villa and wanted to knock on Serita's door. However, he could tell from the darkness beneath the door that she probably slept. All during the day out with the guys, he thought of her. Damien had even brought up that he talked about her all the time, too. He even teased him about falling in love.

Some time later, after Hunter was in bed, he continued thinking about her. Only this time, he envisioned her in erotic poses. His breathing even became heavy and he felt his heart racing. So when he saw his door opening and Serita coming in his room, he almost thought it was a fantasy.

Wearing a white silk gown draped over her curves, she said nothing. She just walked toward his bed, pulled back the covers and got in his bed.

Chapter 13

Serita knew lust possessed her as she entered Hunter's bed. However, it was as if she had no control. All day she had missed him and tonight she ached for his arms to be around her and to further explore his kiss.

Immediately his face came close to hers, so close she felt his heavy breaths on her face. His strong arms sealed her waist against his body at the same instant his butter soft lips pressed hers. Serita's heart hammered like a machine out of control and her arms swept around his shoulders. She savored his hardness.

Soon she felt the tip of his tongue piercing the opening between her lips. Deepening his kiss, Hunter soon thrust his full tongue into her mouth. Tasting his raw, delicious taste, mixed with champagne he had obviously sipped earlier, Serita felt him forcing her down on her back while he leaned over her.

Before long, his hands joined in the pleasure titillating her, roaming gently over her arms, along the sides of her waist and to the curve of her hips. Red-hot tremors raced down to the inner most part of her as his luscious mouth and fingers heated her.

Unable to control herself from her need to touch him, she caressed him as well, her fingers worshipping his arms and chest, and even boldly daring to venture lower on his body. There she felt with overwhelming shock his excitement for her.

"See what you do to me," he slurred between her lips and his.

"Yes," she whimpered. "Oh, yes."

"Keep touching me, baby. Touch me anywhere you want."

Serita continued rubbing the rock hard bulge, making him groan and writhe with excitement. Then she became the happy recipient of his bold exploration. Kissing her hungrier and hungrier, he palmed her breasts through her gown. Serita felt her sensual hunger for him escalating to a level beyond her control. She wanted more, needed more and Hunter soon granted her wish.

Pulling up her gown, he caressed her thighs. All the while, he kissed her deeply as if he couldn't get enough of her kissing. Serita was addicted to everything he did, to everything about him. Yet when she felt him easing his body atop hers, she sat up.

Catching his breath, Hunter asked, "What's wrong, baby?"

Serita liked the way he called her baby. It sounded so sexy, so perfect.

"I'm not ready for this, Hunter."

"Why?" He brushed a tendril of hair from her face.

"Because we haven't known each other that long for one thing."

"But we know each other. I feel like I've known you much longer than we actually have. And you feel that way, too, don't you?"

"Yes."

"So, baby, what's the problem? What's wrong with making beautiful love? With the way I feel about you and the way I sense you feel about me, it will be incredible." He pecked her lips.

Serita felt flutters. "I know it would be."

"So, baby, please."

"Hunter."

"What? Talk to me. You can tell me anything."

"It's…"

"What? You think I'll hurt you?"

Serita cast her eyes across the room, not knowing how to express her inner turmoil.

"Serita, you can't think I'll hurt you?"

She sighed. "I guess it's that we see relationships differently. I just don't sleep with anyone."

"I know. I know you're not like that."

"But if I do sleep with someone, it means that I care deeply for him."

"I know. We care deeply about each other. I feel so grateful to just share your company."

"I feel the same way," she admitted. "But I guess it's that you don't believe in marriage, and committing yourself to someone. You basically just want to have a good time."

"No," he said, cradling her face within his palms. "That's not what I want, especially from you. I love talking to you. I love just being around you. You have no idea and when I'm not around you like today, you are all I think about."

Her mouth inched up in a grin. "Me, too. But I still don't know. I think I better go to bed. I'm sorry if I led you on and I would understand if you're angry with me."

"I'm not angry, but I do admit I want you real bad. But I'll wait. Like I said before, you're worth waiting for."

"Good night, Hunter."

"Good night, beautiful."

Hours after Serita left Hunter's room he re-created their hot encounter. With it, he pondered his dilemma with Serita. He could understand her reasoning for not making love. After all, everyone joked with him about his player ways. Even so, what no one else knew was that he had started feeling something for Serita that he had never, ever felt for another woman. He didn't even know how to describe it. It felt strong, so strong he refused to surrender the idea of making love to her. One of these days, they would make love and it would be a love like neither of them had ever known.

Unable to stay away from Serita, Hunter enticed her out in the coming days to experience all sorts of fun with him. He wanted to become more acquainted with her and let her know that he wasn't just after one thing. So beneath the tropical wonderland of Nassau-Paradise Island, they basked in the sun. Water skiing, boating, shopping, sightseeing, snorkeling and parasailing, they indulged in it all. At the wind up of days packed with overwhelming excitement, they found themselves out on the beach one night. They sat in the sand, enjoying the ocean, the sea and others around them who experienced the shore's splendor.

"I have so much fun with you," she confessed.

"Well you know I feel the same way."

"You know since I've been here on the island, spending time with you, I forgot all of my troubles." She glanced at the waves crashing against the shore, and then gazed back at him.

"You have no more troubles."

She smiled. "You sure make me feel like that. But there are things that will always bother me."

"Can you tell me what they are?'

"Oh, I don't want to bring you down."

"Serita, knowing more about your life won't bring me down. It will make me feel just that much closer to you."

She nodded. "It's about my mother."

"Since you never spoke about her, I thought she passed away."

"No, I feel that she is alive."

"You don't know where she is?"

She shook her head. "No. I haven't seen her since I was sixteen."

"What happened?"

"I don't know. She was the most wonderful mother there was. She made me and my father feel so loved."

"So why haven't you seen each other?"

"It's a long story."

"I'm here to listen as long as you want me to."

She gazed out to sea. "We moved to Madera Bay an island in South Carolina, my home where I live now, from another South Carolina town when I was ten. It had been recently built up as the new vacation getaway and had lots of business due to tourism. My father was an accountant and things were slow where we lived. So he looked into opening up his business there. And it looked good, so he did. And we settled in Madera Bay. Daddy still didn't become rich or anything, but he made a decent living."

"My father went into business, too. I totally understand."

"But my mom was a housewife and she wanted to help bring in money, too. So she got herself a job working as a secretary at a Madera Bay soda factory. It was owned by one of the wealthiest men on the island named Phillip Branson. In fact, my mother worked specifically for him. But my dad was dead set against her working. He had a lot of pride and old fashioned ways."

"Lots of older men are like that."

Serita smiled. "Oh, he was something. But he couldn't stop Mama. Once she set her mind to do something, that was it. And things worked out for a while. Worked out well because mama liked her job and constantly got raises. Plus, her boss always praised her work. But her work skills weren't all that Phillip liked about my mother. I heard Mama telling her friends on the phone how Phillip Branson, a married man, had told her he was falling in love with her. There were other men at the job who had infatuations with my mother, too. Whenever we shopped or dined out, we saw them. Men with lust in their eyes, just ogling my mother. My daddy said it was because she was so beautiful. And she was. She had mixed African and Indian heritage, a beautiful combination."

"Just like you, I bet."

Serita smiled shyly. Yet suddenly her contentment faded. "Some of the women on the island were jealous of her. Whenever she walked by, their husbands couldn't contain their lust. They stared like they could eat her. Those are the same women that talked about her like a dog after everything happened."

"What happened?"

"Phillip Branson had asked my mama to work on some special projects that had her working late hours into the night. My daddy usually picked her up. But on one particular night, my father was sick with a bad cold. Phillip Branson volunteered to drive her home from work. But as the hours passed and passed, and we called the office, we heard or saw nothing of Mama. Sick or not, my father went to the factory. I went with him. The place was closed and locked up.

"So then we looked around the island for her. But we couldn't find her anywhere. We went to the police. And the next night we went to the police again because she never came home. By the third night, the police had a theory for us, but it was the most outrageous thing we ever heard. They said Phillip Branson and two of his friends had seen my mother at one of Branson's cabins on the outskirts of the island. Seen her there after she had left work on her own, saying someone was giving her a ride. They said she was in the cabin with a man. A man that they say she argued with and killed in a crime of passion. They said she ran. They claim they witnessed it through the window. But they lied."

"That's crazy," Hunter said.

"It sure was. They carried the man's body back to town and told everyone that she had murdered the man and fled."

"I'm so sorry, Serita."

Serita blinked back tears. "Most people who

know my mama knew she couldn't hurt anymore. And neither would she cheat on my father.
But those mean, jealous women like Victoria
Branson and her high society buddies, they
called my mother a tramp and murderer. They
dragged her name in the mud. I was even teased
at school by a few bullies. The name calling
eventually stopped as we got older, but the
Branson women always looked at me with spite.
The Branson men were different. Rod was nice
to me. Phillip Branson was, too, even though he
was one of the ones who said that he saw my
mother commit the crime. Every time I saw him,
he looked nervous and went out of his way to be
nice to me. It was strange."

Hunter nodded in agreement. "Indeed it is.
But did you ever look for your mother?"

"Of course. My father spent everything he
had looking for her. We never found her. The
police were looking for her, too. Sometimes, we
wondered if she left us because police were
looking for her. But whatever happened, I know
my mother was a victim just like my Chris was.
And one of these days when I'm financially able
I'm going to look for her and Chris's killers."

"Why don't you let me do it?"

Serita's eyes widened with surprise. "Do what?"

"Let me hire a PI."

"Oh, no."

"Why?"

"I can't do that, Hunter."

"It's not a problem."

"No way."

"Well, at least think about it."

She smiled at him quietly.

"What's so funny?"

"You."

"What's funny about me?"

"Every day I just see a new and beautiful side of you," she said.

"I feel the same way about you."

With that, he leaned toward her and kissed her deeply and lingeringly.

It was a slow day at the station in Madera Bay. Mitchell sat at his desk, poring over the Evangeline Jones files again. As he sat there, he thought of Gilbert Edwards. He wasn't satisfied with the old man's behavior during the last time he questioned him. Hence, he decided to visit him again.

When Mitchell knocked on the door, no one answered. Although he saw someone peek out the window, then move away.

"Gilbert, I saw you," Mitchell yelled. "I need to speak to you again."

The door remained unopened.

"Gilbert," Mitchell called again, this time tapping the window.

Suddenly the door swung open. Gilbert's blue, watery eyes glared at Mitchell.

"I thought I was done with you," the old man said.

"I need to ask you some more questions about the Evangeline Jones case."

"I don't have nothing to say."

"Why?" Mitchell asked mystified. "If you saw a woman murder a man, why don't you want to talk about it?

"Because it's the past. It's dead just like that man she killed."

"I don't know," Mitch said, scratching his temple. "Some things just don't add up."

"Like what?"

"Like Evangeline's blood being at the crime scene. You'll said she took a rock and beat the man in the head with it. But why was her blood there, too? I know you'll told the police because they had a scuffle before she got the best of him, but it just doesn't add up. Plus, from everything I learned about Evangeline, she was a good woman. She loved her daughter and husband and only worked at the soda factory because she wanted to bring in more income and provide for her family. No one ever heard of her having an affair or her being violent."

Gilbert grinned, revealing yellowed teeth. "Think you have it all figured out huh, big-time, big-city detective? Well, before you came, our police had it figured out, and this case was closed and will stay closed!"

"Say what you will, but I just don't get why Evangeline would run away and never come back to a child she loved."

"Because she was a slut that didn't care about nobody."

"I have a different theory."

"What might that be?" he asked bitterly.

"I wonder if it wasn't Evangeline who was killed," the detective said.

Gilbert swallowed and his jaw twitched. Mitchell noted the reaction.

"Wonder what you want," Gilbert lashed out. "I have things to do."

The door slammed in Mitchell's face. Sighing, Mitchell rubbed his hand back through his close-cropped curls.

He thought about Gilbert as he drove down the road and stopped at a gas station. As he filled up his car, he saw Rod drive up to another pump in a new Mercedes.

"Nice car," Mitchell complimented the white, shiny car as Rod stepped out of it.

"Yes, it is." Nodding, Rod admired the car himself and then focused on Mitchell. He stepped up close to him, squinting at him for a long while without saying a word.

Mitchell wondered why he acted so oddly. "You have something to say?"

"Yes, I do. I want to know why you keep bothering my daddy's friend."

Mitchell frowned. "You mean Gilbert? He called you?"

"He called me just as soon as you left. He said you're trying to stir up trouble with that Evangeline Jones mess."

Mitchell was stunned. Why had Gilbert called Rod? He had just left the man. Why did he find it necessary to call Rod and tell him about the nature of their visit?

"The mysterious disappearance of a woman, who was also someone's mother and wife, is not a mess."

"There is nothing mysterious about it," Rod countered. "The woman killed a man and ran to avoid going to prison."

Mitchell shook his head. "I don't think that's how it went."

"Well, how do you think it went, brother-in-law?"

"I'm beginning to think that maybe the lady was killed."

Rod's weathered face filled with a smirk. "You're something. Come here to this island and try to tell our police force they didn't do their job good enough."

"What do you care anyway?"

"Because you're harassing an old man."

"Who you care less about. Now if you don't mind, I'd like to get my gas." He paused, looking at him. "Brother-in-law."

Some time later, when Mitchell walked in the door, he saw Julie sitting on the couch with her arms folded. She looked infuriated.

"What's wrong with you?" he asked.

"You, that's what!"

"What did I do to you?"

"Rod told me about you harassing my daddy's friend Gilbert."

"I wasn't harassing him. I tried to ask him about a case."

"And that's the case you've been talking about since last year—the old case. Why, Mitchell?"

Mitchell observed how upset she had become and frowned. "Why is a good question. Why are you so upset about this?"

"I'm not bothered," she stated, obviously trying to look calmer.

Chapter 14

After a wonderful day with Serita, Hunter strolled along a secluded section of the seashore with Damien. Serita, Lauren and Toni prepared dinner back at the villa, and when the men continuously came in the kitchen because the food smelled so good, the women ordered them out of the house and told them to return in an hour.

"Serita is whipping up that shrimp scampi because I told her that I love that," Hunter gushed. "I think she's trying to spoil me."

"So are you two a couple or what?" Damien

inquired, his chubby cheeks balling up like little apples. "Every time I turn around you two are together. Man I've never seen you get so close with a woman."

"I've never felt this close with one."

Damien reared his head back, gawking at him. "Are you saying you're falling in love with Serita?"

Hunter shrugged, not knowing what to label his intense emotions. "I'm feeling something."

Damien laughed. "Wow, oh, wow. Hunter Larimore has been bitten by the love bug. What's this world coming to?"

Hunter shook his head. "I don't know what it is, but it's driving me crazy."

"She must have really put it on you."

Hunter punched his arm. "You know I'm not telling you my business like that."

Just then, Damien and Hunter spotted an interesting sight in the distance. It looked like two lovers having sex on the beach. Thinking they would get a kick out of spying on them, they strolled near the frisky twosome.

However, as they approached them, Hunter and Damien gaped at each other in shock. Karrin and Greg were naked and writhing in the sand. Once they spotted Hunter and Damien they jumped up and rushed into their clothes. Hunter and Damien waited a minute allowing Karrin to get herself presentable, before they marched over to them.

"I can't believe you two!" Damien yelled.

"Me, either," Hunter added.

"Oh, please," Karrin spat. "You're just jealous."

Hunter chuckled at that. "Jealous of what?"

"Because I've found a real man instead of you."

Greg beamed. "Hey, man, we couldn't help ourselves."

"You're a fool," Hunter told him.

"Forget you," Greg snapped.

"I agree with Hunter," Damien piped in.

Karrin sucked her tooth. "Screw both of you. You both want me!"

Damien laughed out loud.

Hunter glowered at her. "You are just no good. Toni is as nice as can be to you and you betray her by sleeping with her man."

"So!" Karrin propped her hand on her hips. "She should take care of her man's needs, so he won't have to go to someone else who can."

To that, he just stared at her and then switched his irritated expression to Greg.

"And how could you do that to Toni?"

"Toni doesn't understand me. Doesn't understand my needs or anything else."

"Then what are you marrying her for?" Hunter asked.

"Yeah, why am I?"

Disgusted, Hunter strode away and threw his hand at them. Damien trailed him, his face showing equal disgust.

"I'm not thinking about that ugly mess," Hunter said. "I'm going to the house and get my grub on. If he wants to throw away a pearl for a pebble let him."

"I hear you, man," Damien concurred.

Later that evening, Sierra lay in her bed, sleeping and dreaming of Hunter, which made her smile. In the dark, Hunter walked toward her, preparing to make love to her. Yet suddenly within the blink of an eye, he vanished. In his place another man stood—a man with a ski mask who held a knife.

With her head turning from one side of the

pillow to the other, Serita willed herself awake.
No one stood above her. Still she felt frightened.
She couldn't be alone. She hurried to Hunter's
room and, like the time before, slid into his bed.

"I had a bad dream," she told him.

He kissed her cheek. "Well, it was just a
dream. You're here with me now."

She caressed his face. "Make me feel better."

"Oh, I can make you feel like you never felt
before," he promised and kissed her lips.

Serita's body burned where he touched her.
Then as he glided his smooth lips across hers,
he grabbed her, drawing her body close to his.
Since he wore only silk pajama bottoms, Serita's
fingers worshipped every inch of his chest and
arms with gentle caresses. And when he slipped
his tongue in her mouth, she tasted more
luscious than the last time he kissed her.

Swirls of raw heat crowded the base of her
stomach. Serita wanted him more than ever.
Hearing her body's cry, Hunter slid her nightgown off her body. Before she knew anything, he
had her out of her panties, too. For a second, his
eyes soaked up her naked body hungrily. Then
hurriedly he took off his pajamas. All the while,

he gazed at her body as if starved for it. Once naked he made Serita gasp and want him even more.

In a second, he put on a condom, and then quickly positioned himself on top of her. Instantly Serita wrapped her arms around his hard back and felt his rock hardness wedge into her naked flesh. Hunter's tongue delved deeply in her mouth, greedily draining her of her honey before he lowered his head to her chest.

The silky wetness of his mouth on her breasts made Serita tremble with delight. Increasing his pleasure, he squeezed her buttocks and nudged his hard length even deeper into her. When she thought she could take no more of the ecstasy, he lavished her with more. While flicking his tongue across her nipples, he moved her legs apart.

Just the tip of Hunter drove her wild. Inch-by-inch, he thrust into her, letting her relish every inch of him that filled her. With every motion, Serita felt like she lost herself deeper and deeper in a sea of pleasure. Smelling him, kissing him, holding him, she welcomed him inside of her. Then finally he gave her himself fully. He pushed deeply within her as far as he could, moving in and out and ravishing her with erotic moves. Serita lost her mind, swaying her hips in time with the sensual rhythm of his.

His love was addictive and she never wanted it to end. Nothing had a right to feel so good, Serita thought, savoring the sweetness of his tongue seeking hers and drenching her face, neck and breasts with red-hot kisses. Hunter kissed her more deeply and with each kiss, he deepened his thrust down inside her. The ecstacy caused her to scream at the top of her lungs. She couldn't get enough of him. But as their fire grew so hot that neither could stand it, Serita knew she couldn't hold on to this rapture forever. She felt the ultimate joy and knew he did as well. Their muscles contacted together and they collapsed on each other spent and sweating.

After thinking of what Hunter must have thought of her, Karrin decided to give him one last try. She headed to his room and knocked. When he didn't answer, she cracked the door. Although the room was pitch black, the moonlight shed a little light in it. Hunter lay sleeping with Serita snuggled in his arms. She saw from her bare shoulders sticking above the covers, that Serita was naked. Hunter had made love to her. Karrin burst into tears and fled down the hall to her room all the while thinking how much she hated Serita.

Chapter 15

After falling asleep within Hunter's arms, Serita woke and stared at him. He slept peacefully and looked so handsome that she couldn't resist pecking his cheek. He stirred in his sleep. She couldn't resist pressing a kiss on his lips. He stirred even more. She continued her exploration on the rest of his body.

Peeling back the covers, she kissed his chest and lower to his belly button. Soon Hunter smiled and opened his eyes lazily.

"You're fresh, girl," he said in a voice laden with sleepy huskiness.

"You're the one."

"Umm umm umm, you showed me all kinds of moves."

"Stop," she said, tapping his chest.

"You drove me crazy."

"You did the same to me."

He stared at her, mingling his fingers in her hair.

"You have pretty hair."

"Thank you."

"You have pretty everything," he said with a naughty laugh.

"You're bad, Mr. Larimore."

"And I want to get even badder with you again. But first I have to tell you something." He studied her quietly. "I feel something with you that I have never felt with any other woman."

"You really do?"

"Yes, I do."

"That makes me feel really good. Because I feel something really special for you, too."

With that, she climbed on top of him. He welcomed her, caressing the sides of her hips and she leaned down to him kissing him deeply. On and on their lovemaking went for hours. Hunter pleasured her body in every position imaginable. Repeatedly there were knocks on his door, but Serita and he ignored them. They preferred to bask in the afterglow of their closeness.

When she prepared to leave because they all had tickets to a concert and she had to dress for the event, Hunter clung to her.

"I don't want to let you go."

"I don't want to let you go, either, handsome, but Damien and Lauren bought those tickets to do something nice for us and we have to go. It would be rude not to go."

He sighed lazily. "I'd rather be in bed with you."

"I want the same, but we do need to give our bodies a rest."

"I don't need rest. I need you. I meant it when I said I've never felt this way before. No other woman has made me feel like this. Only you. Feel my heart." He took her hand and placed it on his chest. The wild hammering beneath her hand almost alarmed her.

"See what you do to me."

"You do the same to me, but I better go," she said.

"Wear something sexy for me."

"I will."

Serita opened his door to leave, hoping no one would see her leaving his room in a nightgown. Yet as soon as she closed the door, she saw Karrin leaned against the wall. Serita could tell that Karrin was fuming.

"Hello," Serita greeted her.

Karrin looked her up and down. "Mighty late in the day to have a nightgown on."

"Well, I'd better get dressed, then." Serita made a step in the direction of her room.

Karrin blocked her path. "Don't think you're special."

"Excuse me."

"You heard me. Don't think you're special."

"Have I done something to you?"

"Oh, don't act innocent."

"What are you talking about?"

"I'm talking about that man in there!" She pointed to Hunter's room.

"What about him?"

"He told me the same thing."

"What?"

"Told me no one made him feel like that just to get me in bed."

Serita's eyes bulged. "You were listening to us?"

"I was coming to his room to ask him something and overheard."

"No, you eavesdropped."

"I have better things to do with my time. Besides, I'm just telling you so you know you're not special."

"Please, you're just jealous."

"I'm not hardly jealous. He's been trying to get me in bed, but I'm seeing someone else."

"Yes, another woman's fiancé. I heard what you're doing and it's low."

"Who cares what you think?"

"No, you don't care what I think but you do care what I do with Hunter."

"I could have him again if I wanted."

"You're pitiful," Serita said and walked away shaking her head. Serita didn't glance over her shoulder, but she swore she could feel Karrin's eyes burning a hole into her back.

Mitchell sat at his desk in the Madera Bay Police Station, sorting through paperwork while his mind drifted miles away. He couldn't stop thinking about Julie's harsh reaction to his re-opening the Evangeline Jones case. With it, Rod's response to his questioning his father's friend seemed bizarre. As well, Gilbert's reluctance to discuss what happened continuously nagged him. Everything in his gut told him something had gone awry and Serita's mother, Evangeline had been the victim, not the criminal.

Thinking about it all, his mind wandered to Serita. Perhaps he needed to stop by her house and tell her about his instincts. Then again, he needed to wait and get more information before he roused her hopes. If her mother had been killed, at least he could clear her name as a murderer. Moreover, he could punish the true murderers. Perhaps one of them killed the deceased man.

As Mitchell thought about this, one of his colleagues, Kevin, came into his office and dropped a file on his desk.

Mitchell examined the file and soon looked up at his freckled friend who he often talked over his problems with. "You mean to tell me that the Chris Johnson that was killed last year did not have a criminal record?"

Kevin sighed and shook his head. "The computer somehow mixed up his file with another Chris Johnson. That Chris Johnson had a rap sheet."

"And the Chris Johnson that Serita Jones married never had a police record?"

"No, he never did."

Dazed, Mitchell pondered his mistake. "Thanks for letting me know."

"Sure," Kevin threw over his shoulder as he strode away.

Mitchell clutched his face and rubbed it harshly. It was as if he wanted to wipe all the tension from his brain. Yet he couldn't wipe his mistakes away. He had to tell Serita that he had been mistaken. It also made him wonder about the case. She insisted that Chris hadn't tried to kill her.

Seconds later, Mitchell pulled the files to the case. He pored through every detail until he read something that he hadn't paid attention to when the murder first happened. The serial numbers were filed off the gun, so it had never been traced to who registered it. It all brought questions to Mitch's mind.

Why would a guy who shot his wife in a heated moment and then killed himself dropping the gun right between them, file the serial numbers off ahead of time? Gunmen filed off serial numbers when they tried not to get caught. So why would a man committing suicide make the effort to do so? He wouldn't, Mitchell answered in his mind. Perhaps Serita had been right. Perhaps Chris Johnson had not shot her or committed suicide. Perhaps a murderer lurked among them.

Mitch headed out and hopped in a squad car headed to Serita's house. When he pulled up in the driveway, he saw her neighbor Mrs. McFee outside gardening.

She stood, reared back, rubbing her lower back, and then beckoned him over.

"How are you today?" Mitchell greeted her.

"I'm all right. Gardening relaxes me."

He glanced at her colorful, fragrant garden. "It's very nice."

"Why, thank you. And I'm glad to see you. I called the station and talked to someone, but they didn't seem to care."

"Talked to them about what?"

"The man I saw looking around Serita's house. Isn't that why you're here?"

"A man?"

"Yes, one night I heard noises. It was dark and I saw this guy in dark clothes peeking around looking in the windows."

"This is the first I've heard of this."

"I yelled at him, asking what he was doing but he ran off."

"Can you describe him?"

"No. It was too dark, and my eyesight isn't that great. But he couldn't have gotten in anyway. Serita had an alarm installed before she left."

"Left?" His head lurched back with shock. "Left for where?"

"Nassau-Paradise Island in the Bahamas."

"She's on vacation?"

"Her girlfriend and hubby hit the mother lode with some business project and treated a group of their friends to a summer in the Caribbean. Isn't that nice?"

"Yes, real nice," he said, his mind fuzzy with this news. "When will she be back? I need to talk to her about some things."

"She's supposed to be gone for the whole summer."

"Do you have information on how I can reach her?"

"Yes, I do," Mrs. McFee said looking uncomfortable.

"Well, can I have it?"

"I'm sorry, Detective. Serita instructed me not to give out her information."

"But this is a police matter."

"You sure it isn't a personal one?" Mrs. McFee eyed him suspiciously.

"It's both. I care about her."

"Care a little too much for a married man, don't you, Detective Lane?"

Hours later Mitch headed to his bedroom and saw Julie sitting in bed reading. Back when they lived in Chicago, he would always find her in bed reading a mystery novel. He loved those, too, and they would always talk about the book. But things were different now. She was different now. Lying across the bedspread were business reports Rod had dropped off at their house that morning before he left.

Mitchell sat on the side of the bed and loosened his tie. "How is your father?"

"The same." With her brows furrowed, she looked up from a stack of papers. "I just pray."

"Me, too." He undressed silently for a few seconds, and then asked, "Why don't you read novels anymore in your spare time?"

"Because Rod and I are trying to keep all that my father worked for from falling apart."

He reflected on her answer. "You used to care about more than making money."

"I still do care about lots of other things."

"You're turning into a workaholic who's obsessed with making money, just like Rod."

"Is it wrong to want to be comfortable?"

"No, it's not wrong."

"Especially in light of the children we now have."

"I can take care of our children."

"I know you can, but I still like having extra security." Sighing, she shoved the papers aside, placing them on a night table. "I don't want to talk about this or the Evangeline Jones case. I just want to be with my husband. I want him to make love to me." She eased across the covers on her knees and placed her chin in the crook of his shoulder. "You haven't touched me in a while."

"Because it's hard to make love to a woman you don't know."

"What do you mean? You know me?"

"No, I don't, Julie. All you think about is money."

"And all you think about is Evangeline Jones. Now why is that? Why is it that you're so pre-occupied with a murderess?"

Mitchell didn't bother to answer her. It would have led to an argument. Hence, he stood and walked to another room.

Chapter 16

"Man, you two can't beat me," Hunter declared, entering the villa bouncing a basketball.

Damien dragged his body in behind him and flopped down on the couch.

Greg ambled in after him. "Ah, you cheated, man." He plopped down on the chaise.

Hunter bounced the ball in the midst of them. "Don't you know by now that basketball is my game?"

"Well, if you're such a hotshot," Greg said,

"why don't you play some of those teenagers down there on the court?"

Hunter tucked the ball beneath his arm. "Oh, man, lighten up. I'm just having a bit of fun. And I'm not about to try and beat a teenager. Shoot, I'll be glad just to run around on the court with them a bit."

Just then, Karrin flitted into the room and eyed Greg seductively. "Hello, there."

"Hey yourself, beautiful," he said hurrying over to her.

Hunter and Damien shook their heads in disgust.

"Where is Lauren?" Damien asked her.

Karrin played with a strand of her hair. "Toni, Lauren and what's her face went shopping. You just missed them."

Hunter eyed her with annoyance. "Why do you have to refer to Serita like that? You know her name."

"I'll refer to her any way I want."

"What are you so mad about?" Damien asked.

"None of your business," she answered and focused on Greg. "What are you doing the rest of the day?"

"Well I was going to take a shower."

"Why don't we shower together?"

Greg flashed nearly every tooth in his mouth. "Oh, yes. Yes, yes, yes."

She headed to her room. Greg followed eagerly. Once they were out of sight, Hunter looked at Damien, not hiding his revulsion.

"What the hell is going on with him?"

Damien shook his head. "A severe case of being whipped. I've never seen Greg act so stupid, and I've seen him very stupid before."

"I hear you. But forget him. If he wants to mess up his life, it's his life to mess up."

"This is true."

"I'm going to go hop in the shower and then let's go out for grub. I have a taste for some of that conch."

Because Toni had forgotten her credit cards, Serita and Lauren accompanied her back to the villa nearly an hour after they left it. As Lauren and Serita rested on the sofa, Serita made a mental list of the things she wanted to buy. At the top of her list was a gift for Hunter, maybe a cute shirt or a bottle of cologne.

But just then, they heard a commotion coming from the side of the house where the bedrooms were located. The yelling and screaming propelled Lauren and Serita up from their chairs and down the hall. They fled into Toni and Greg's room where the ruckus was coming from.

To their astonishment, Toni and a naked Karrin fought, tumbling across the room. Every now and then, Greg tried to run between them and stop the battle. Each time he did, the fighting women knocked him out of their way.

"Stop it!" Lauren yelled.

"Please stop before someone gets hurt!" Serita added.

To that, Karrin glowered at her. When she did, Toni slugged her, knocking Karrin flat on her back on the floor. She lay there winded and unable to get up. Greg ran to her, helping her stand.

"Are you all right?" he asked.

"Yes," Karrin answered breathlessly. She grabbed her long T-shirt and slipped it over her head.

"I can't believe you would do this to me!" Toni yelled at Greg. She shifted her glare to Karrin. "And you! You're supposed to be my friend!"

Karrin sucked her tooth. "Oh, please, I can't help it if you can't satisfy your man and he had to come to me to take care of his needs."

"Huh," Toni huffed. "You mean he went into the garbage to get the trash!"

Karrin smirked and raked her eyes over Toni. "Don't hate on me because I'm fine as hell. Isn't it obvious why he chose me over you?"

"Hell, no, it's not obvious!" Lauren threw in.

"Thank you," Toni added.

"Aw, you two are just jealous 'cause I look so good. Toni, look at me and look at you. No wonder Greg looked elsewhere."

"You're smut!" Toni snapped.

At that point, footsteps approached the room. Before long, Hunter and Damien joined the others.

Hunter scoured the ransacked room, looking astonished. "What the world went on in here?"

"What's going on?" Damien asked, looking at a disheveled Toni and Karrin.

Karrin propped her hands on her hips and looked at Toni smugly. "I took her man, that's what! And she walked in on us."

Hunter went to Toni and put his arms around her. "I'm sorry, hon. You don't deserve this."

"Damn right, I don't," Toni yelled in a shaky voice as tears formed in her round eyes.

"You're a damn fool!" Hunter shouted at Greg.

Greg's small eyes shriveled. "Mind your business, Hunter!"

"I want you two out!" Lauren stated, dividing her glare between Karrin and Greg.

Karrin looked Lauren up and down. "Hell, I'm grown and I'm not going anywhere."

Damien stepped toward her, cracking his knuckles as he walked. "Yes, the hell you are getting out. We paid for this trip and we want your bony tail out! Now!"

Karrin backed down, shuffling behind Greg.

Greg looked at Damien. "Well, we're leaving together. We'll be better off so we can have some privacy."

Being so humiliated and disrespected Toni bolted from the room.

Hunter frowned at Greg. "Aren't you going after her?"

"I feel bad for Toni," Greg said blankly, "but I'm with Karrin now."

"Fool!" Lauren yelled. "Big old fool!"

Greg twisted his mouth sourly. "Yo, Damien, you better check your woman."

"I'm not checking nothing! You are a fool and I want you out now! Get your junk and both of you get out!"

"Fine with me," Karrin said. "It's too crowded in this house anyway." With that, she rolled her eyes at Serita.

Once Greg and Karrin had packed and left, Serita and everyone else rallied around Toni and attempted to comfort her. Yet Toni was heart-broken. Days later, she decided to leave the island. Wanting to support her, Lauren and Damien left with her.

After Serita and Hunter saw them off at the airport, they returned to an empty house. Although Hunter disliked what happened to his friend, Toni, he loved the idea of being alone with Serita in the villa.

They spent the day experiencing nothing but pure bliss. They played checkers, watched cable movies and listened to slow jams. They ate and after they stuffed themselves, Serita sat on Hunter's lap and asked for dessert.

"I have some dessert for you, all right," he teased her, coasting his hands along the sides of her hips.

"You do?" she said playfully.

"Oh, yeah."

Chapter 17

"Now I have you all to myself," Hunter said after they had entered his bedroom. He sat on the side of the bed with Serita. "I could get used to this."

"You could?"

"Oh, yes. You have me thinking things that I never thought about with any other woman."

"Like what?"

"All kinds of beautiful things, like babies."

She gasped. "Are you for real?"

"I'm more serious than ever. I feel so much

for you. I'm even overlooking what happened years ago."

"What do you mean?"

"I had a friend, a best friend. I met him at college right before I met Damien and Greg. He was a great guy, smart, funny, goodhearted and sensitive. Too sensitive in fact for his own good. He met this girl, and he just fell for her. Lost his mind he was so crazy in love. And she played with him, made him think she loved him, made him think there was no one else. Then one day he came to her place and found her in bed with another guy.

"She laughed in his face and told him it was over—just like that. He tried to get her alone to talk, but she didn't want anything to do with him. For days he tried to get with her, but she rejected him. Then one day I came home from class and he had a gun in his hand. I tried to get away from him, but he wouldn't let me have it. He just told me to tell his folks he loved them, and then blew his brains away."

"Oh, God, no."

"Right in front of me. You know, I've never told anyone before you that I witnessed what happened."

"Oh, baby, maybe that's why you were so afraid of love."

"It definitely affected me. I said that no one would get that close to me. But I learned since I met you that you can't tell your heart what to do. It loves who it wants." He stared at her quietly. "And I love you, Serita. I can't believe these words are coming out of my mouth, but it's true. I didn't want to fall in love and make myself vulnerable to all that pain that love brings, but I can't help it. I love you so much."

"Oh, Hunter," she said, caressing his face. "I love you, too."

With that confession, Serita watched Hunter stand above her and lift his T-shirt over his head. His broad, bare muscled chest shimmered and when he came down on the bed, she couldn't keep her hands off of it. Lustful aching grew low in Serita's belly. Within seconds, Hunter had on a condom and had her out of her clothes. Soon he kissed her, touched her soft fruit, playing with her nipples and then entered her.

"It feels so good inside you," he slurred against her mouth before moving in and out and duplicating the motion with his tongue in her mouth and later rocking her fiercely with an erotic motion the was all his own. When the pleasure felt so good that both of them screamed from the intoxicating feeling they realized they couldn't hold on to paradise forever. They collapsed in each other's arms with Hunter lapping up the juices from her lips.

Mitchell sat in the lounge of Madera Bay General Hospital while Julie, Rod and Victoria paced. The doctor had called them because Phillip Branson's condition had worsened. When the doctor came out into the lounge everyone crowded around expecting the worse.

"No, don't be alarmed," the gray-haired doctor said. "He's just asking to see one of you."

Rod stepped forward. "I'll go. I need to talk to dad anyway."

"No," the doctor said, and gazed at Mitch. "Mr. Branson wants to see his son-in-law."

Rod gazed at him with shriveled eyes. "You sure he didn't say his son?"

"I'm sure. He said he wants to see Mitchell."

Moments later, Mitchell stepped into Phillip

Branson's room and saw the old man's faint smile. Phillip beckoned Mitchell to sit next to the bed. Mitchell complied and sat next to him.

"How are you feeling, Phillip? Are you in pain?"

"I'm not in pain," he said weakly. "Just weak and tired."

"You're getting the best care. Hopefully you'll be able to go home one of these days."

Phillip's dried lips inched up in a grin. "I don't think so."

"Oh, don't say that."

"Forget me. I called you in to tell you something."

"Sure go ahead, Phillip."

"It's bothered me for years. And I can't go to my eternal rest without getting it off my chest." Tears welled up in his eyes. "It was so wrong."

Frowning, Mitchell leaned toward the bed. "Phillip, it's okay. Just take your time and tell me."

"It was so wrong. I—"

"Mr. Branson," the doctor said. "It's time for an exam." The doctor looked at Mitchell. "I think he's had enough visiting for today."

"But I have something to tell him," Phillip insisted.

The physician patted Phillip's arm. "Tomorrow."

Mitchell retuned to the cafeteria. Only Rod remained in it.

"Where's Julie?"

"Her and mama went to the lounge," Rod answered. "What did daddy want with you?"

"He wanted to talk to me about something."

"Something like what?"

"Why are you so interested?"

"Because you're not getting our money."

Mitchell chuckled. "Money didn't even come up."

"So what did?"

"Why are you so concerned?"

"If my father is telling you something on his deathbed, I have a right to know what it is."

"Just get out of my face."

"I'm not going anywhere. You're cozying up to my dad trying to get ahead of me in this family. But I have a good mind to tell him what his son-in-law has been doing behind his daughter's back."

Mitchell's eyes narrowed at him. "I have no time for you."

"You sure had time for Serita Jones. I know about your cheating behind my sister's back! I've seen your car at her place. Seen it there for hours. What were you doing, police business?"

Mitchell wanted to tell him something. Yet just then, Julie and Victoria walked up. Mitchell kept silent. So did Rod.

On Nassau-Paradise Island, Serita and Hunter made the island their play land indulging in all sorts of fun activities and enjoying the villa alone. One night as they danced the night away at the Palm Club, they ran into Karrin and Greg. Serita noted that Greg looked downhearted, or maybe she imagined it.

"How are you doing?" Hunter asked Greg.

"I'm all right. How are you two?"

"We're great," Serita answered.

Karrin's nostrils flared. "Where is the rest of the crew?"

"They left."

Greg frowned in surprise. "They went back to New York?"

"Yes," Hunter responded.

"What about Toni?" Greg pressed. "How is she?"

Karrin reared back and glared at him. "What the hell are you talking about her for?"

"Because we were going to be married," he answered testily.

"So!"

Greg sighed with irritation and looked at Hunter. "It's good see you two out and together."

Hunter smiled at Serita. "It feels good, too. I can proudly say that the love bug has bitten my butt big time."

Serita smiled at him.

Karrin rolled her eyes.

Hunter stared at Serita. "And I mean that, baby, sincerely from my heart," he said and kissed Serita lightly on her lips.

"Wow," Greg said beaming at them both. "Serita, you're some woman to make this man admit he is in love."

Serita smiled.

"Well," Hunter said, "have a good night, folks." He strolled away with his arm around Serita's waist.

Shortly after, in the ladies' room, Serita leaned toward the mirror inspecting her makeup. Because she danced so much, some of it had sweated away. She blotted her face with a tissue and felt refreshed. When she turned to leave, Karrin blocked her path.

"Hunter doesn't love you."

"Karrin, get out of my face."

"You two staged that to make me jealous."

"I don't have to do anything. Jealousy is all you are."

With that, Serita walked around her and left the ladies' room.

Chapter 18

Serita and Hunter made love all over the villa after they returned from the Palm club. They ended their hot time in her bedroom and then slept for hours. When Serita woke, she felt famished. However, they had been enjoying themselves so much over the last days, they never had time to shop. The refrigerator was empty. So were the cabinets. She wanted to order in, but didn't know who stayed open at such a late hour.

"I'll go get us something," Hunter said after he woke and learned about her hunger.

"But it's so late."

"I don't mind. I'm rested anyway. You just lie there and I'll bring something back."

"From where?"

"Don't you worry."

He kissed her on the forehead, dressed and left the villa soon after. Serita stayed in bed, not only basking the afterglow of their lovemaking, but thinking about the wonderful man who had come into her life. Smiling, she drifted off to sleep.

Serita began dreaming again about Hunter approaching her bed. She stretched her arms out to him. Then suddenly he transformed. The man wearing a ski mask appeared. Serita tossed and turned forcing herself to wake. Though, when she opened her eyes, someone did actually stand above her bed.

Her heart banged with alarm. A masked man approached. He carried a knife. Serita screamed and ran. He caught her as she neared the window hoping to run out of it. Then suddenly she heard other fast footsteps and his grip loosened on her.

She swung around. Hunter battled with him until the knife stuck in the man's stomach. Holding it as it protruded from him, he then fled out the window. Hunter dashed after him. Serita dialed the police. Hunter returned shortly after.

"I couldn't catch the animal. He hopped into a car. Are you all right, baby?" He embraced her.

"Yes."

"Oh, God, he could have hurt you."

"But he didn't. Because you saved my life. Thank you."

"I forgot my wallet and came back for it. Thank God that I did."

After the island's police finished speaking with Serita and Hunter, they promised to investigate the matter. They also claimed the man might have wanted to rob the place or rape Serita. Serita then made them aware of what happened a year earlier. They took notes and found her information interesting.

"It was just like my dreams," she said.

"Don't worry, this animal will be caught. We won't leave."

"So you know what this means?"

"What?"

"That the person who killed Chris was

stabbed. I know that's who that was. I can feel it. I just don't know why he's after me. What have I done?"

Chapter 19

When the doctor called Mitchell at the police station and summoned him to the hospital, he expected to also see Julie, Rod or Victoria there. Instead, the doctor expressed that Phillip Branson specifically didn't want them to come. He only wanted to see Mitchell.

When Mitchell walked into the room and sat next to him, Phillip wasted no time in unburdening himself.

"It's about Evangeline Jones."

"Somehow I suspected it was."

He took a deep breath. "She was so beautiful. I couldn't help myself from staring at her whenever I saw her. It made my wife so jealous of her. She used to call her a tramp. But she wasn't."

"What is the real story, Phillip?"

"One night she worked late for me as my secretary in the administrative offices of my soda factor. Gilbert dropped by and my other buddy. They had been drinking. They were also staring at Evangeline as she worked, saying things they shouldn't have to her. I should have stopped them. But I didn't.

"I had told her I would take her home since her husband was sick that evening. They rode along. Gilbert and Cedric got in, too. But I didn't take her home. Gilbert and Cedric whispered in my ear and told me to take her to my cabin. Evangeline sensed something awry and begged me to please take her home. But I didn't. I listened to them. We took her there and…"

"You raped her?"

"No, but I wanted her. But not that way."

"So what happened?"

"Gilbert and Cedric they held her down and they did it—they raped her.

"I told them to stop. God, how she screamed. But they kept on and on over and over again. Then a man heard her screaming."

"John Winston, the murder victim?"

"Yes."

"He caught them in the act and did what I was too much of a coward to do. He pulled them off her. But Gilbert managed to get a rock from out back. He bashed his head with it."

Mitchell sat quietly as the old man confessed.

"Blood went everywhere. We knew he was dead."

"But what about Evangeline?"

"She witnessed it all and tried to run. Gilbert hit her with the rock too and knocked her out."

"So he killed her?"

Phillip shook his head. "No. We thought he had. But after we loaded John Winston's body in the car to dump him in the ocean, we came back for Evangeline. She was gone."

"So she escaped?"

"I don't know how. She was out cold. He hit her so hard with the rock."

"Then what happened?"

"We searched for her. If she went to the police

our lives were ruined. So we knew we had to get to them first. We took John's body to the police and said we caught her in my cabin, seducing him then killing him after they argued. The authorities called it a crime of passion."

"That's horrible."

Tears seeped down Phillip's cheeks. "We ruined that woman's life and killed a man all because of our damned lust."

"So where is Evangeline Jones?"

"I have no idea. But I have wondered where she might be, or if she is alive every day. My conscience killed me, so I told my wife and children."

Mitchell's mouth dropped open. "You did?"

"Yes, Rod, Julie and my wife, Victoria, know. They know the whole truth."

Mitchell sat stunned. "I can't believe this."

"Believe it." Suddenly his faced hardened with rage. "They were the ones who made me keep silent all these years. They begged me to never tell. So did Gilbert and Cedric. I hated them all because of this. That's why I did what I did."

"What did you do?"

"That poor girl."

"Who?"

"Serita Jones. She had to live without her mother. She had to live with folks saying her mother was a killer and with people like my wife turning up their noses at her. And it was wrong. I grew up without a mother. It's an awful feeling. One of the hardest things in the world. That's why I changed my will.

"My selfish children will each have one small company to run. My selfish wife will have the mansion and $100,000. But all my businesses and my multimillion dollar fortune is willed to Serita Jones."

"My Lord. Does anyone else know?"

"My son found out when he overheard me changing it when I called my attorney to my home. He begged me to change it. I told him I never would."

An hour later, Mitchell stormed into his house. He searched for Julie in the house and found her out on the patio. She looked furious.

"I have something to discuss with you," he said.

"I have something to say to you, too!" Her voice filled with rage.

"You knew about Evangeline Jones."

"What are you talking about?"

"You knew the real story, Julie. Your father told me it and how your mother, you and Rod talked him out of doing the right thing."

"He did no such thing!"

"I just came from the hospital."

"You shouldn't be harassing him about that."

"He called me to the hospital. He wanted to get this burden off his chest. How could you!"

"How could I what?"

"How could you go on with your life encouraging him to let this poor woman be blamed for something like that. Maybe if someone had told the truth, she would be with her family right now."

"You mean she would be with your precious Serita."

Surprise widened his eyes.

"Yes, I know, Mitchell. I've known for a while now." Tears filled her eyes. "You went behind my back and slept with that woman! And so many times when I passed her house I felt like going into her house and blasting her away in her bedroom, too."

Mitchell gasped and his eyes literally bulged from their sockets. "My God!"

"What? I didn't do that."

"Then how did you know she was shot in her bedroom?"

"Because. Because Rod told me."

"How did he know that?"

"From the papers or news I guess. Why are you asking?"

"Because we specially didn't tell anyone where Serita and her husband were shot. We withheld as much of the crime details as possible and that was one of the things that we didn't tell the media."

"Maybe someone on the force told."

"No, Rod knew because he was there."

"Have you lost your mind? My brother is no killer."

"And it makes sense."

"How?"

"Your father has willed the bulk of his estate to Serita."

She gasped. "He did what?"

"Rod knows about the change in the will."

"My brother is no killer."

"He is! Where is he now? Home?"

"No."

"Then where?"

"I'm not telling. He is no killer!"

He grabbed her shoulder and shook her. "I need you to tell me. He'll kill Serita if you don't."

"No, he wouldn't."

"Tell me."

She broke down and cried. "I had mentioned that I saw Mrs. McFee in the salon and she told Serita's beautician that she went to Nassau-Paradise Island. When I mentioned Serita to Rod, he said he wanted to get her straight about messing in my marriage."

Mitchell grabbed his suitcase and opened it.

"Where are you going?" she asked.

Frantically he grabbed his clothes from the drawers.

"Where do you think? Serita is in danger."

Hunter rented a car, so Serita and he could tour the island at their leisure. One night as they drove, they wound up in a remote area. For miles and miles, the rented vehicle remained the sole one on the highway until he saw a black SUV. He spotted it in his rearview mirror speeding down the road. When it neared their vehicle, he expected it to pass them. Instead, it sped so fast

and so straight that Hunter wondered whether
the driver was drunk or ill. It appeared the other
car meant to drive them right off the road.

All of his speculations flew out the window
when she saw the jeep drive up beside his and
bump the car. Serita and he shouted at the driver,
who they couldn't see behind black tinted
windows. Hunter also stepped up his speed. It
did no good. The next thing he knew, the maniac
rammed into the back of his car so hard that it
swerved off the side of the road. Quickly Hunter
maneuvered the wheel or otherwise they would
have smashed into a tree.

"My God," Serita screamed.

"My God, is right. Baby, what is going on?
First, that animal at the house, now this."

A few nights later, Hunter relaxed in the
villa's living room while Serita went to her room
to telephone Lauren. A suspense thriller played
and he hoped Serita would hurry up and get off
the phone because he knew she enjoyed that
genre of movies, too.

But just then, a knock on the door surprised
him. Thinking it might be the police with information about the attacker that broke in, he

looked surprised to see Greg at the door. He looked somber.

After Hunter invited him in and they relaxed on the sofa, Greg took a deep breath.

"You were right about Karrin."

"I told you."

"She's awful. And she was just using me to make you jealous. She's so obsessed with you and Serita she can't speak of anything else."

Hunter sighed. "Sorry, man."

"Hey, you tried to warn me. It wasn't even fun anymore after we left the house. She acted as if I irritated her. All she did was complain and criticize everything. And then when I couldn't afford to buy her something, she told me I wasn't a real man."

"That's Karrin all right," Hunter said.

"She even flirted with guys in my face. It got to the point I couldn't stand her and I didn't want to touch her. She didn't even look the same to me anymore. I hate that I messed up with Toni."

"Toni is a good woman. She stuck by you through all your problems."

"She sure did."

"Well, I feel I have me a good woman, too."

Greg smiled. "You two are tight, huh?"

"Oh, yes. I'm even going to take the big step."

Greg's eyes stretched. "You're not saying what I think."

"Oh, yes, I am. I'm going to ask Serita to marry me."

"Congratulations. My man is turning in his player card."

"For good."

Suddenly Greg became deep in thought. "You know, I really came by because of Serita."

"What's up?"

"One night when Karrin and I were out we saw this guy at the bar in this club, showing a picture of her. He had got it from some news clipping."

"News clipping?"

"I suspected it had to do with when she was shot."

Hunter speculated. "Interesting."

"Yeah, I thought so, too. He didn't seem right. I wasn't about to tell him I knew her, but Karrin did."

"Oh, no."

"Oh, yes. She even told him Serita was staying here during her vacation. Karrin thought he was a boyfriend looking for her, but I think it was something else. He was weird."

"What did he look like?"

"Baldheaded dude. Not that good-looking. Average."

When Greg left, Hunter sat absorbed in his thoughts. Because of the odd happenings, they were scheduled to leave tomorrow night. The departure couldn't arrive soon enough for him, especially in light of what Greg told him. Someone was after Serita and he had to keep her safe. In fact, he had made arrangements for her to come back with him to Virginia. He would never let her out of his sight. A killer was on the loose.

Chapter 20

On the last day of Serita's trip to the island, she almost hated to leave. Though scary incidents had taken place, more wonderful ones had made up for it. She couldn't believe that she had fallen in love again—fallen in love with a man so dreamy that at times she wondered if everything that happened was real.

As Hunter showered, preparing to get dressed for their flight, she wanted to take one last look at the beautiful surroundings. She drifted through the lovely rooms of the villa, and even wandered outside. A forest stood nearby it and she walked toward it in hopes of getting the last drops of tropical air and exercise.

Wandering through the wooded area, she wished she had spent more time here. It was beautiful with lush palm trees and several clear-water ponds. Yet as she stepped deeper into the area she thought she heard footsteps behind her. She turned around to see if anyone else roamed the area. But she saw no one. A few steps further, she heard the sound again. The steps sounded clearer and clearer, but the person who made them remained out of sight.

A funny feeling fluttered over Serita. She started thinking that in light of recent incidents she shouldn't have taken such a chance. She turned around and stepped briskly back toward the villa. Just then, a familiar face emerged from behind a tree.

"Rod?" she said frowning at her fellow islander. Of all the people to see, his appearance shocked her.

He smirked. "That's right. Rod Branson at your service, Ms. Serita Jones. You know, you're just as pretty as your mother. And you affect men the same way. Make them forget their sense and become controlled by lust. But I have other intentions."

Serita's heart skipped a beat at Rod's strange words and menacing manner. "What are you doing on this island?"

"What do you think I'm doing here?"

"I have no idea."

"I came to see you, of course." He took a step toward her.

She took a step back. "Why?"

"To protect what's mine."

"I don't know what you're talking about."

"It's nothing personal. Wasn't even personal last year when I came into your bedroom."

Serita gasped. "Came where?"

"That night when you cooked for your hubby. I was just protecting what was mine."

Serita clutched her mouth, sobbing into her palms. "You killed Chris? You killed my Chris? Oh, my God! Why? He didn't even know you! He didn't do anything to you!"

"Neither did you, but I had to protect what was mine."

She cried. "What are you talking about?"

"My daddy. He willed you his fortune. The only way I can get it is if you're dead."

"What? What you're saying is crazy. Why would he do that? Why are you doing this?"

Rod whipped out a knife. "Like I said it's nothing personal. I actually like you."

"Please." Serita backed away.

"I'm sorry, but I love money, always did."

"Please, God."

"My God is money."

Rod lunged at her, but Serita eluded his grasp and ran.

Hunter had looked all through the house for Serita when he heard someone knock on the door frantically.

"Yes," he said swinging the door open.

"I'm Detective Mitchell Lane from Madera Bay."

Hunter looked startled. "From Madera Bay?"

"I received Serita's address from her neighbor, Mrs. McFee. I need to see her."

"Why?"

"To save her life. A man is after her."

* * *

Breathing hard, Serita stopped running. She couldn't run anymore, though she could still hear footsteps and she knew Rod wasn't far behind.

"Serita," he yelled. "I'm going to get you, darling! I will."

"No, you won't!"

Suddenly Serita was shocked again. Mitchell appeared with Hunter. Hunter grabbed Rod and fought with him. When Rod tumbled to the right, Hunter punched him until he lost consciousness. Mitchell stepped in and handcuffed Rod and tied him to a tree. Once Rod was secured, they walked toward her. Hunter reached Serita first and swallowed her in a hug.

"Baby, how could you leave the house like that after all the scary incidents?"

"I just wanted to soak up my last moments on the island." She cried on his shoulder. "Oh, God, he tried to kill me and he killed Chris. But I don't understand it all." She gazed at Mitchell. "Do you know why he did it?"

"Yes. His father was supposed to drop your mother home one night after work. But they took her to a cabin…and the other two…"

He dropped his head.

Serita shook her head. "Oh, no."

"A man came and saw what they did and tried to stop it. That was John Winston."

"The man who was murdered. The man they said my mother murdered?"

"They knocked him over the head with a rock and killed him. Then they bashed your mother with that same rock."

"Oh, God, no!"

"But she didn't die, Serita."

Serita's eyes widened. "Then where is she?"

"I don't know. They couldn't find her and feared she would tell what they did and ruin their lives, so they hurried to the police first and concocted a story about her. They claimed that she killed Winston and fled, and everyone believed them."

"My God."

"That's inhuman," Hunter remarked.

"It is. And what makes it worse is that Phillip Branson was consumed with guilt. He wanted to confess, but his family wouldn't let him."

"Who told you this?"

"Phillip Branson himself. He said he had no

mother and it felt so awful that he felt for you and despised his selfish children. That's why he put you in his will."

"What?" she exclaimed.

"You are to receive the bulk of his multimillion dollar estate. The only way Rod could get it is if you died. And he feared you getting it because his father is gravely ill." He eyed Rod on the ground. "But you won't have to worry about him anymore."

Hunter walked over to Rod and said, "Nope, she sure won't."

The next day after Rod's arrest Mitchell stood in the airport with Serita while Hunter took care of their flight arrangements to Virginia.

"It looks like you're leaving Madera Bay," Mitchell said.

"Have to. I need a new start."

He nodded. "I know what you mean."

Serita studied him. "How do you feel about Julie now knowing she encouraged her father to hide his horrible crime?"

"I have no feelings for her. In fact, I've

decided to look into getting custody of our children and divorcing her."

"I hope everything works out for you."

"For you, too." He glanced at Hunter, who stood at the ticket counter. "He seems like he loves you a lot."

"I know he does. I feel the same way."

He pondered that. "I can't blame him. I love…" He hushed and stared at her a moment. "I apologize about Chris. I'm sorry I told you he was a criminal, because he wasn't. I'm sorry I didn't believe you when you said he wasn't a murderer."

"Your apology is accepted. Now I have to go. Goodbye, Mitchell."

"Goodbye, Serita."

Days later, Serita had settled into Hunter's luxurious Virginia home. She had also just returned from meeting his big, happy family. As they snuggled on the sofa, she smiled.

"Your family is so nice."

"They are not," he teased. "Those people are crazy."

"No, they aren't. They're sweet like you."

"You think you can put up with them?"

"Of course."

"What about for the rest of your life?"

She eyed him curiously. "What are you saying?"

He gazed in her eyes tenderly. "That I love you. And I want you to be my wife. Will you marry me, Serita?"

Her eyes filled with tears. "Oh, baby, yes. Yes."

With that, they kissed passionately and he led her to his bedroom.

Lying on the bed together, Serita welcomed him kissing her face all over until his lips worked his way to hers. There he his mouth glided across hers before his tongue explored the honey beyond her lips. Serita clasped her arms around his broad shoulders. While she did, she felt his hands coasting along the sides of her tiny waist.

Tremors of red-hot need welled up in the pit of her stomach as soon as he disrobed. Tantalizing caresses pampered every curve that she had. All the while kisses delighted her lips and soon her breasts. As his warm mouth treated her nipples to long moments of attentiveness, her excitement grew unbearable. And when he stroked between her silky patch, she quivered from the overwhelming sensations of pleasure. At every titillating moment, he whispered in her ear how much he loved her. Kissing him, feeling him, smelling the coconut oil that entranced her senses, she whispered that she loved him, too.

Unable to withstand not being one any longer, Hunter put her legs around his waist and she hooked her arms around his neck. A breath later, she felt his hardness pushing so deeply inside her and then rocking her with erotic moves that were all his own. Ecstasy rushed down to the inmost part of her as the pleasure grew intolerable. She tightened her feminine muscles to hold him within her forever. But soon their love grew too hot to bear. Their bodies shook. Their moans saturated the air. And they collapsed within each other's arms, breathless, sweaty and spent.

Chapter 21

After spending a blissful time together and taking a needed rest, Hunter woke up and watched Serita sleep. Because they became sweaty after lots of lovemaking, her rich, dark skin looked as if it had silk oil poured over it. Her long locks looked wild, spilling over the pillow. Her features looked so sensual that they beckoned his lips to kiss each one of them. He did it so delicately she never awakened.

It amazed him that this beautiful woman wanted to spend the rest of her life with him. He

knew it would stun the family when they heard
the news about the marriage. They had held off
on sharing the good news because they were
still toying with the idea of eloping. But a crucial
matter had to be taken care of first.

He couldn't let Serita wonder about her
mother's whereabouts. Finding Evangeline
Jones took precedence over all else at this
moment. That's why he had hired the finest
private investigator in the state of Virginia.

Days later, Hunter received the spectacular
news that Evangeline Jones resided in South
Carolina merely two hours away from Madera
Bay. When he shared the news with Serita, she
gawked at him in disbelief.

"Are you sure she is my mother?"

"The guy I hired is the best, baby. If he says
he found her, he found her. Tomorrow we're
flying in my plane to see her."

"Oh, my God. It will be such a miracle to see
my mother again. It will be such a blessing."

The next day a taxi pulled up in front of a
small, white frame house in a deserted area of
Summerville, South Carolina. Serita and Hunter
stepped out of it. Immediately the multicolored

flowers blooming in the garden captured her attention. Still, as she gazed about the surroundings, she saw a poorly maintained house. Paint peeled from the exterior and the screen door nearly fell off its hinges. As Serita knocked, her heart broke knowing that her mother had not only been brutalized, and forced to escape a wrongful prosecution she had also been forced to live in such poverty.

"May I help you?" a frail woman asked. She appeared to be in her eighties and she gawked at Serita as if something about the young woman startled her.

Serita looked equally startled. The woman that stood before her looked nothing like her mother. Moreover, she looked to be the age of Serita's deceased grandmother.

"Miss, we're sorry to trouble you," Hunter said. "But we're looking for this woman." He pulled out a photo of Serita's mother.

The woman accepted the photo and examined it closely. A slow smile formed on her parched lips. Then she raised her gaze to Serita's face. "You're Ann's daughter. The investigator said you would be coming. You look like she spit you out. That's why I stared. You resemble Ann so much."

"Ann?" Serita said, "Why do you call her Ann?"

"She'll tell you why. Come in." She widened the door for their entry.

Like the outside, Serita saw that the homes interior needed many repairs. Overall, though, the living room looked neat, clean and had cozy, earth toned furnishings. And when she led Serita up a flight of stairs to the second level, the decor equally pleasing. When she led her to a bedroom and opened the door, the women inside had her back to Serita, straightening a picture on a wall. Yet Serita's racing heart had already told her that her mother stood there before Evangeline Jones even turned around.

Serita gasped. Her mother looked not a day older, except for the slivers of gray in her hair. She smiled at Serita with tears in her eyes. Serita reacted in the same way. They rushed toward each other, joining in a hearty embrace.

"Mama?"

"Serita. Serita, you're just as I remember you."

Hunter marveled at the reunion while the elder woman stood in the doorway. Her face filled with contentment.

Serita reared back from her mother. "Mama, there are some things that happened to you that I will ask you about. But first, I want to know how you wound up here."

"I had amnesia. The doctors say from a head wound. But I never forgot you. I always saw your face and knew I had a child somewhere. I prayed every night that we would get back together."

"And we did."

"Ms. Betty here found me floating in some waters while she fished."

The older woman nodded. "She had passed out and had a big gash on her head. I took her to the hospital here and they said someone had struck her hard enough to kill her, but she didn't die. Thank God."

"And I couldn't remember anything, except your face. And I had no way of finding out who I was. I had no money, nothing. So Ms. Betty took me in. And since I didn't know my name, she called me Ann."

"And she's been my daughter ever since. I loved every moment of taking care of her. Now I'm sad. I know she's going to go."

The older woman talked on. Hunter stood back listening and thought about something that he could do to make this happy ending even happier. Days later, he flew Evangeline and Ms. Betty back to Virginia. The reason being, he had purchased them a house that stood right next to his own. Serita could now see her mother every day. They could also have their privacy.

Days after settling the two women into their home, Serita lay in bed with Hunter basking in how wonderful everything had turned out.

"Mama and Ms. Betty love their new home."

"I'm so glad."

"You should have seen them in the home goods store today buying all of these curtains and spreads and everything to hook the house up. They're having so much fun decorating it. It's so much more beautiful than the home they lived in."

"Yes, it is," Hunter said.

"Thank you for everything. Sometimes I just can't believe you're real, Hunter Larimore." She kissed him long and lingeringly. When she left his embrace, she noticed him eyeing her oddly.

"What's going on in that brain of yours?"

"Us."

"What about us?"

"We're eloping."

She gasped with excitement. "When?"

"Tonight. I let it slip to my brothers earlier on the phone, but they've promised not to tell anyone."

Chapter 22

"We're home," Hunter whispered into his bride's ear as he carried her into his house. "Now I really have a home."

"And it's going to be a sizzling-hot one tonight," Serita promised. Hunter carried her up into his bedroom and she saw rose petals spread over his leopard spread. Gently he laid her on them.

"You told me you were romantic the first night I spent with you," she said, gazing up at Hunter.

With his lust-drugged eyes never leaving hers,

he unbuttoned his tuxedo shirt hastily. "Just hold on, baby. Just keep it hot for me. I'm going to give you some loving that's going to make you smile when you think of me and even if you just hear my name."

Serita laughed and reached out for him. "Come, bring it to me, lover."

"Hunter?" an alarmingly familiar high-pitched woman's voice called from outside. Hearing it, Hunter froze and looked at Serita as if the intruder signaled the world ending.

Serita sat up, her jaw dropped. "Baby, who was that? It sounded like somebody's grandmother."

"Oh, God," he uttered.

"Who is she?"

"My Aunt Essie May."

Serita looked tickled. "She's coming to see you on your wedding night? That's so cute."

"Cute nothing! I shouldn't have told my brothers anything. Those big mouths must have told everybody. I bet the whole family knows we eloped."

"Hunter," the high-pitched voice uttered again. "Boy, don't let me get one of these switches out here in these bushes and take it to your butt. You better not ignore your auntie just because you all in love."

Hunter clutched his forehead. "Why me?"

"'Cause she loves you like I do," Serita said, scooting to the edge of the bed. "Now go see what she wants."

"But, baby, you got me all…"

"Hunter, you know that's not nice just to ignore your auntie."

"All right." Hunter took a deep, exasperated breath and buttoned his shirt back up. He hurried down to the front door with Serita trailing him. When he opened the front door, Aunt Essie May's wholesome body greeted him with a hug.

"I knew it. I've seen it. I've seen you married in my visions. And I told you. You didn't believe me. You believe me now, boy?"

"Yes, Aunt Essie May," Hunter said with a laugh. "You got me. You were right."

When she let go of him, she stepped over to embrace Serita. She gazed at her, shaking her head. "My brother and his wife told me you were beautiful, just beautiful in every way." She embraced her tightly. "Welcome to the family child. You two will make beautiful children."

Once Aunt Essie May stepped back from Serita, Hunter expected her to go on home and let them get the honeymoon underway. Yet not only did she pass through the door, but the entire Larimore clan poured in. Hearing the commotion next door, Evangeline and Ms. Betty joined in the celebration, too. Before long, all kinds of delectable aromas of food floated through the house, along with great love songs. All the while, Hunter's parents fussed at him about eloping. But they also embraced Serita welcoming her to the family.

His brothers teased him about his player days being over. His sisters informed Serita that she had married the most irritating Larimore man there was. He was the family's prankster. Though all in all, everyone had a fabulous time. Even Hunter's six-year-old niece, who never bit her tongue, found her uncle's marriage amazing and entertaining.

"Uncle Hunter, you finally found someone to rock your world. Your bachelor days are over."

Hours later, the family had gone and Serita lay snuggled within Hunter's arms.

"I can't believe this." He spoke softly.

"What? That we're married?"

"No, that I found you. In this big old world, I found someone so precious and special that I fell in love. God sent you to me out of everybody in the world. I'm so lucky and so blessed."

She pecked his lips. "I feel the same way, baby."

"And believe me I'm not ever letting you go. You're locked in. Can you handle that?"

"I can handle anything as long as you're by my side. I thank God for you, Hunter Larimore."

"I thank God for you, too, baby. I thank him so much for bringing you into my life. I love you," he said, saying once again the words he'd sworn he would never say to a woman.

"I love you, too," Serita said.